Her unorthodox proposal—a paper marriage to suit them both—had seemed eminently sensible.

She wanted a husband to discourage suitors, smarmy men and endless chat-up lines. He wanted a wife to dissuade women from thinking they could be the ones to change his heart. A woman he genuinely liked, who didn't want to love or be loved by him, made *sense*. Here was someone he could get along with, who would make no demands, who would be interesting company when he chose to have it. The idea of such a marriage had seemed to suit them both, and he'd never actually regretted it.

But what on earth did his wife want now?

"Well?" he prompted when it seemed as if she wasn't going to say anything. "What is this oh-so interesting proposal of yours?"

"I want..." Lana took a gulping sort of breath, very unlike her, before she steeled herself and met his gaze with her own, blue eyes bright with determination, chin tilted upward. "I want to have your baby."

After spending three years as a die-hard New Yorker, **Kate Hewitt** now lives in a small village in the English Lake District with her husband, their five children and a golden retriever. In addition to writing intensely emotional stories, she loves reading, baking and playing chess with her son—she has yet to win against him, but she continues to try. Learn more about Kate at kate-hewitt.com.

Books by Kate Hewitt

Harlequin Presents

Claiming My Bride of Convenience
Vows to Save His Crown
Pride & the Italian's Proposal
Back to Claim His Italian Heir

Passionately Ever After...

A Scandal Made at Midnight

One Night with Consequences

Princess's Nine-Month Secret
Greek's Baby of Redemption

Visit the Author Profile page
at Harlequin.com for more titles.

Kate Hewitt

PREGNANCY CLAUSE IN THEIR PAPER MARRIAGE

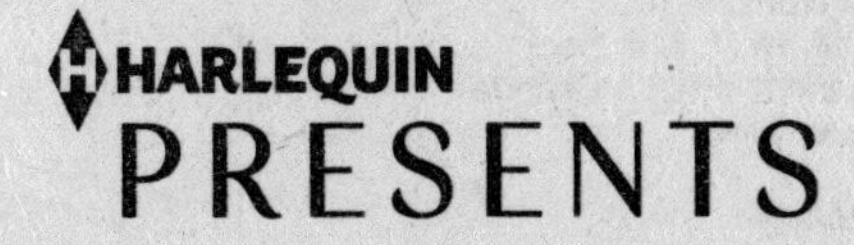

ISBN-13: 978-1-335-59329-0

Pregnancy Clause in Their Paper Marriage

For questions and comments about the quality of this book, please contact us at CustomerService@Harlequin.com.

Harlequin Enterprises ULC
22 Adelaide St. West, 41st Floor
Toronto, Ontario M5H 4E3, Canada
www.Harlequin.com

Printed in U.S.A.

PREGNANCY CLAUSE IN THEIR PAPER MARRIAGE

CHAPTER ONE

LANA SMITH MOVED purposefully through the well-heeled crowd, her ice-blue gaze skimming over the elegantly coiffed heads of the top echelons of New York City's business world. Socialites rubbed elbows with bankers, lawyers, and entrepreneurs, while the strains of a seventeen-piece orchestra swelled over the tinkling sound of laughter and the clink of crystal. Among all these rising and shining stars, she could not see the man she was looking for, the man she rarely looked for, but desperately needed right now.

Her husband.

'Lana!' Albert, an aging tech wunderkind who had availed himself of her company's PR services a year ago in order to rehabilitate his somewhat sagging reputation, came towards her, hands outstretched, to air-kiss her on both cheeks. Lana made the requisite kissy noises before leaning back and smiling at him, trying not to appear as distracted as she felt. *Where* was Christos? Earlier that day, he'd texted her that he'd be here tonight. She'd been on the fence about attending at all, because it was her fourth function in the space of a week, but it was always helpful for the two of them to make appearances, short and sweet, together. That wasn't, however, why she was looking for him now.

'I saw your husband just a short while ago,' Albert told her, and Lana's gaze narrowed as her heart leaped.

'You did?' She took a sip from the crystal flute of sparkling water she held in one hand, trying not to sound as eager as she felt. 'Let me guess. Holding court in the whisky bar?'

Albert gave an indulgent chuckle. 'How did you know?'

'Christos always prefers a smaller, more captive audience,' she quipped, although she wasn't sure that was entirely true. Her husband of three years was still something of an enigma to her, and rightly so. She hadn't been particularly interested in getting to know him, beyond the basics, and he'd felt the same. Their convenient marriage had suited them both; they had a healthy respect for one another as well as a pleasant, unthreatening affection and camaraderie, and that was all that was needed for a successful marriage.

Until now.

'I probably should go say hello to him,' Lana told Albert, with a smiling roll of her eyes. 'We've been like ships passing in the night these last few weeks.' Last few years, but nobody actually knew that salient fact, which was, essentially, the point of their marriage.

'Don't be a stranger,' Albert called after her as she began walking towards the ballroom's doors. 'I have a friend whose image needs a little polish…he's young, up and coming, but awkward. You know how it is. I mentioned your name.'

Lana turned back to give him a quick, laughing look. 'You know how to find me,' she replied with a flick of her long, poker-straight strawberry-blonde hair, and then she kept walking, her head held high, a faint smile on her lips as she nodded at the various guests she knew or at least recognised.

She'd been part of this crowd for nearly ten years, first as a wannabe hanger-on when she'd started as a lowly administrative assistant for one of the city's top PR firms, still trying to figure out who she was, then rising to consultant, and then, as much out of painful necessity as ambition or desire, starting her own firm six years ago, having left behind a career—and a heart—that had taken a brutal battering. For a second she let herself remember those years, when she'd been so young, so impressionable, so *broken*, all thanks to one man.

But, she told herself, she could give credit where credit was due—if Anthony Greaves hadn't broken her heart and stamped on her pride, grinding it nearly to dust, she might never have started her own business…or married Christos Diakos.

Marrying Christos three years ago, New York City's enigmatic tech investor and once considered its most eligible bachelor, had been the icing on the cake, cementing her success both in society and business. Not that she needed a man for that, of course, but Lana certainly understood the need to be pragmatic.

Which was what tonight was all about. She'd explain her new plan to Christos in the same businesslike terms in which he'd agreed to their marriage, and that would be that. Yet the clenching of her insides, the sudden speeding up of her heart, told another story.

Somehow Lana didn't think this was going to be as easy or simple as she wanted—and needed—it to be. Even after three years of marriage, she couldn't say she really knew her husband or how he'd react to the proposal she was about to put to him, but she did know that despite his laughing wryness, his easy manner, he had a core of absolute steel. He hadn't swept into this city and taken over business after business, held his nerve with some of the riskiest investments imaginable, and risen to multimillionaire status all within a few years on charm alone, although he had that in spades, as well.

At the imposing double doorway of the ballroom, Lana paused, taking a breath to steady herself, flicking her hair once more behind her shoulders, straightening her spine. The pale blue evening gown she wore, a simple sheath of satin, matched her eyes and made her stand out like a column of ice, which was exactly the image she'd tried to go for when she'd reinvented her broken-hearted self at age twenty-three—sophisticated, a little bit remote but ultimately approachable, determined but also charming, which was why she smiled at everyone she saw, without letting it *quite* meet her eyes. She'd spent a long time cultivating the right image as a PR consultant, someone who had to be both aspirational and approachable, friendly yet always professional. Besides, a sense of reserve came naturally to her, after a turbulent childhood and a single, disastrous romance; it was like a layer of armour against the slings and arrows of the world, one she knew she needed.

Yet she sometimes had the uncomfortable, prickling suspicion that her husband saw through that carefully constructed façade—although to what underneath, she couldn't say. *That* she knew she never gave away, not to anyone, and never would, not even to herself. She'd left that lonely little girl, that broken-hearted woman, behind a long, long time ago.

With her chin tilted at a challenging angle, Lana headed into the hotel's whisky bar, a carefully curated den of masculinity, with deep leather club chairs, a mahogany bar, the amber shades of a hundred different whisky brands glinting in their bottles behind it.

She saw Christos immediately, her gaze instinctively drawn to his magnetic presence, picking him out from half a dozen men with ease. He was that notable, that charismatic, sprawled in a leather chair, a tumbler of whisky dangling carelessly from his fingertips. Dark, rumpled hair, a little too long, a powerfully lithe body well over six feet, so he stood head and shoulders over most men in any room. Golden-green eyes that often looked sleepy, but Lana knew better; he'd be taking in everything. He'd probably leave this so-called social meeting with several business tips, or even a contract in the making. That was one of the things she admired about him. One of the things that had made him, for her, husband material.

She took a step into the bar and waited for him to notice her. Another thing she admired about him—he didn't play games. Didn't pretend not to see her for some stupid ego boost, the way so many men did. The way Anthony had, his gaze skimming over her with something like malice as she'd watched him chat up another woman.

No, Christos turned as soon as she stepped into the room, his gaze training on her like a laser, making an unexpected heat bloom through her body, a quickening of her pulse.

She'd long ago trained herself not to react to that gaze, often seeming sleepy yet so intent, or that powerful body, the muscles of his shoulders rippling under the starched white cotton of his button-down shirt. She didn't react to the bergamot scent of his aftershave, or the long, relaxed stride he had, like a lion who didn't even need to pounce. Chemistry, never mind actual sex, had never been part of their bargain, and that had been for a very good reason.

And it wasn't going to be part of it now, despite what she was about to ask him. Again, Lana's insides clenched with nerves. Did she really want to do this? Did she dare? She'd had three days to think about it, three days to absorb, accept, grieve. Three days to weigh the pros and cons, to try not to feel emotional, even though she knew, deep down, that this was entirely an emotional decision. One from the heart, the kind she'd learned never to make.

Yet here she was.

'Lana.' Another thing she had learned not to respond to—Christos's voice. Rich and deep, and always with a hint of laughter. Not mean-spirited laughter, the mockery of a man who needed to feel superior—and goodness, but she knew what *that* sounded like—but the genuine humour of someone who found the world a fun place to be. Utterly unlike her in some ways, but Lana liked it about him. He relaxed her, maybe without even meaning to.

She inclined her head, let a smile curve her lips. 'Christos.'

'Sorry, gents, matrimony calls.' Christos rose from his chair in one fluid movement. Despite his height, or perhaps because of it, he was a man who moved with easy grace. He tossed back the last of his drink in a single swallow before handing the glass to the bartender with a fleeting smile of thanks. Yet another thing she liked about him—he was always kind to staff, to the people others would have seen as utterly irrelevant and beneath them.

All evidence, she told herself, that she was making the right decision now.

Christos strolled up to her, stopping close enough so she could breathe in his aftershave, feel his heat. Her stomach contracted again, as much with awareness as with nerves. Lana had steeled herself against a response to him over the years, but occasionally it still came up and surprised her, a sudden wave of longing she did her best to suppress. She didn't need that kind of complication. Now she tilted her head up to meet his laughing gaze.

'You wanted to speak to me?' he asked, his tone turning momentarily serious, his hazel gaze scanning her face with a concern that made something in her soften.

'Sexy and nice,' an acquaintance had once told her with a laugh. *'How did you get so lucky?'*

Of course, that woman hadn't known the truth behind their marriage.

'How did you know?' she asked.

He raised his eyebrows. 'You only look for me at a party when you want something.'

Lana tried not to flinch at that rather matter-of-fact assessment. It was true, but it made her sound a bit like a grasping shrew, not that he'd said it in a mean way, far from it. 'Well,' she said mildly, lowering her voice so others couldn't hear, 'that is the reason for our marriage.'

'Well I know it, my dear.' His tone was teasing, without any spite or malice. Christos had always taken their paper marriage in his stride; he'd been remarkably unfazed when, at an event like this one three years ago, Lana had suggested the idea to him. She'd done so with a calculated sort of recklessness, expecting it to shock or maybe amuse, but Christos had merely raised his eyebrows, smiling, and asked for details.

'Are we meant to be on show,' he asked as he slid his arm through hers, 'or is this a private conversation?'

'Private,' Lana replied as her throat suddenly went tight. She really had no idea how Christos was going to react to her suggestion.

'Very well,' he replied equably, 'but we might as well take a spin around the room for form's sake, don't you think? I don't believe we've appeared in public together for a couple of weeks. You wouldn't want people to start talking.'

'I'm not sure it matters, after three years,' Lana replied as he gently steered her from the bar, back to the crowded ballroom. 'Surely by now our marriage is an accepted fact in this city.'

'Ah, but people always like to speculate,' he replied, leaning down to murmur in her ear so his breath tickled her cheek. Lana stiffened, doing her best to ignore the tingling sensation that little whisper had caused to spread through her whole body, a spark she forced herself to instantly suppress, before it could ignite. Now, more than ever, she did not want to complicate things between her and Christos with an intense physical reaction. Besides, she was pretty sure she was reacting to him this way, after three years of learning not to, only because of what was on her mind. Her heart.

And she had no idea how Christos Diakos, her *dear husband*, was going to take it.

* * *

Beneath his arm, Lana's was as taut and hard as a rod of iron. His lovely wife was often tense, although she did her best not to show it, but tonight the cracks in her usually indefatigable armour were starting to appear, at least to him. Christos doubted anyone else at this party saw beneath Lana's polished and icy façade. She made sure they didn't. She'd done her best to make sure *he* didn't, and for the most part she convinced him that what he saw with her was what he got. But occasionally, like now, when she was clearly trying so hard, he wondered what lay beneath that cool smile and steely gaze.

Hoped, even, that there was something soft and warm underneath? He mused over the possibility before discarding it with deliberate determination. No, not hoped, not at all. Lana might have convinced herself she'd drawn up their terms of marriage, but Christos had been the one to approve the contract. He wouldn't have agreed to anything he didn't want to, and one absolute necessity of their so-called union was that emotion didn't come into it at all. For Lana, certainly, and also, absolutely, for him. So, it didn't matter what was beneath her all-business demeanour, because the truth was he didn't actually care. He would never let himself.

They'd done three sides of the square ballroom before Christos decided he was too curious about what she wanted to bother to complete their stroll. He reached for two flutes of champagne from a circulating tray, only to have Lana shake her head firmly and heft her own glass.

'I've already got a drink.'

He arched an eyebrow as he took in her half-drunk flute of Pellegrino. 'Water?'

'I want to keep a clear head.'

Lana rarely drank alcohol for just that reason, but she was still partial to the occasional sip of champagne. With a shrug, Christos took only one flute. He was becoming more and more curious what his wife needed to speak to him about, because it was clearly something. Something urgent.

Did she want a divorce? Or in actuality, an annulment? He considered the possibility with a necessary dispassion. Part of their agreement had been the understanding that either one of them could end it when they saw fit—when it no longer suited them, or if they fell in love with someone else.

Had Lana fallen in love? His stomach tightened rather unpleasantly at that notion. No, surely not. He would know. He knew his wife far better than she thought he did. Even though they saw each other somewhat infrequently, she couldn't keep that kind of thing from him. Still, it was clearly something, something that would change things between them in some way, and he wasn't about to waste any more time figuring out what it was.

With Lana's arm clasped firmly in his and his flute of champagne in his other hand, he shouldered his way through the crowded ballroom to one of the hotel's smaller salons along the corridor—one of those impersonal, elegant side rooms rented out for business meetings or intimate receptions. The one he chose was empty now, but it had clearly been used for a meeting earlier in that day, because there was an easel with a whiteboard propped on it in the corner, with a heading in dry erase marker half wiped away.

Three Points Regarding...

Lana saw it the same time as he did, and they shared a small smile, both of them having been in many such interminable meetings. Christos slipped his arm from hers, tossing down his champagne before discarding the flute on a side table as he strolled towards the board.

'Have you got three points for this discussion?' he asked, taking the whiteboard marker and holding it poised above the board, as if to write them down. Lana looked startled, and uncharacteristically discomfited.

'Wha—what?'

She really was not on form this evening, he mused, which was very unlike her. Why not? 'Three points regarding whatever it is you're going to propose.'

'How do you know I'm going to propose something?' she asked, her voice only slightly unsteady.

Christos turned to face her. 'Because you marched into the bar to find me, you want to have a private discussion, and you're nervous.' He smiled faintly. 'There, those are my three points—three points regarding my wife's intent, whatever it is.'

She let out a small, somewhat reluctant laugh. 'Very astutely observed, Christos.'

He inclined his head in wry acknowledgement. 'I try.'

'I know.' She paused, looking straight at him, and Christos felt—something—in him contract. Squeeze. Lana Smith was a stunningly beautiful woman. Tall, elegant, slender, strong. Her hair fell in a gleaming sheet of blonde with a hint of auburn halfway to her waist, not a strand of it out of place. Her eyes were the colour of blue diamonds—pale without being watery, fierce and gleaming in a face that could have graced a Greek statue—of Athena, perhaps, rather than Aphrodite. There was too much strength of character in the clear lines of her face for it to be reduced to some sort of insipid beauty. Her body possessed curves in all the right places—lush yet lithe, supple and graceful. He'd always admired how beautiful she was, as well as how focused and driven, having built her business from nothing six years ago, and worked hard to get it to where it was, one of the city's top PR firms, specialising in the rehabilitation or reinvention of significant figures in the business world.

Christos tossed the marker back on the easel. 'So, what is it you want to discuss with me, Mrs Diakos?'

She looked as if she wanted to protest the name—she'd stayed with her maiden name of Smith for professional reasons—but then she gave a little shake of her head instead.

'I do have—a proposal.'

He folded his arms, took a studied stance. 'As I thought, then.'

'It won't actually affect you that much.'

'Which potentially makes it all the more intriguing. Or, possibly, completely uninteresting and depressingly dull, depending on what it is. I assume you're not asking for a joint credit card?'

She wrinkled her nose, unable to keep the flash of proud disdain from her face. In the three years of their marriage, she'd never asked him for money. She'd been the one to insist on a prenup. 'No.'

'You want my Netflix password?'

She rolled her eyes, a smile tugging at her mouth. He'd always liked how he was able to amuse her, even when she was trying not to let him. *'Christos.'*

'Hulu, then? No? Well, it's a good thing, because since we live in separate residences that's strictly forbidden.'

Her smile deepened, and it felt like a triumph.

'All right, then.' He raised his eyebrows. 'What is it?' He really was curious now. Why was she so nervous? She hadn't been this unsure of herself when she'd proposed, three years ago, while they'd been sitting at a bar much like the one they'd just left.

He'd been slouched on a stool, minding his own business, ruefully reflecting on the woman who had only just kept herself from throwing her drink in his face, simply because he'd decided their liaison had come to an admittedly swift end, as he always did. He never made it past three dates, never got to the point where emotions could be engaged. It was a rule that had served him well, despite the histrionics, which were admittedly tiresome. At that point, he'd been ready to swear off women for good, which was why, perhaps, he'd been willing to listen to Lana.

She'd slid next to him on the bar stool, ordered a Snake Bite—whisky and lime juice—and tossed it back in one swallow. Already he'd been impressed—and intrigued.

'Tough night?' he'd asked, and she'd slid him a speculative, sideways glance, looking worldly-wise and weary even though she hadn't yet turned thirty.

'Considering I hate half the human race, you might say so.'

He'd let out a surprised laugh at that. 'Likewise, but I think I hate the other half,' he'd told her. 'What happened to you?'

'Just the usual,' she'd replied, holding up her hand for another drink. She'd shaken her hair over her shoulders, her expression turning to iron. 'Some smarmy man thinking he knows better than me simply because of what he's got in his pants. Condescending to me in business and copping a feel on the way out. What about you?'

He'd been briefly enraged on her behalf, although she'd shrugged it aside as if it happened every day, and maybe it did. Suddenly his own frustration—that a woman had taken a break-up badly—had seemed both petty and arrogant in comparison.

'I can't say likewise this time,' he'd told her ruefully. 'Just that I narrowly avoided having a drink thrown in my face.'

'Well, as long as you avoided it,' she'd replied

dryly, and he'd laughed again. He *liked* this woman, he'd realised. He'd never met another woman like her.

A couple of drinks in, her unorthodox proposal—a paper marriage to suit them both—had seemed eminently sensible. She'd wanted a husband to discourage suitors, smarmy men, and endless chat-up lines. He'd wanted a wife to dissuade women from thinking they could be the ones to change his heart. A woman he genuinely liked, who didn't want to love or be loved by him, had made *sense*. Here had been someone he could get along with, who would make no demands, who would be interesting company when he chose to have it. The idea of such a marriage had seemed to suit them both, and he'd never actually regretted it.

But what on earth did his wife want now?

'Well?' he prompted when it seemed as if she wasn't going to say anything. 'What is this oh-so interesting proposal of yours?'

'I want…' Lana took a gulping sort of breath, very unlike her, before she steeled herself and met his gaze with her own, blue eyes bright with determination, chin tilted upwards. 'I want to have your baby.'

CHAPTER TWO

TO HIS CREDIT—or not—Christos's expression didn't change. He simply regarded her thoughtfully, his deep green gaze scanning over her slowly, while Lana tensed, waiting for his reaction, his response. She wasn't going to jump in with all her explanations and caveats, her assurances and reassurances, as much as she wanted to. Not until she could gauge his response to what admittedly appeared to be an outrageous suggestion. Although not, she reminded herself, as outrageous as it might first seem, once she'd explained.

'Well, this *is* interesting,' he finally remarked in a low, lazy drawl. 'Definitely more interesting than a joint credit card. Even more so than sharing Netflix. *Much* more, as it happens.'

'I'm serious, Christos.' Her voice trembled and she made herself take a steadying breath. She usually enjoyed and appreciated his ready sense of humour, but she wasn't sure she could bear him joking about this.

'Yes, clearly you are.' His laughing look dropped

as he cocked his head, his gaze still sweeping over her in assessment. 'In fact, I don't think I've ever seen you so serious before, Lana. Not even when you first proposed to me.'

'That started out as something of a joke,' she protested, a bit feebly. They'd both been more than a little drunk at the time, restless and reckless from their recent, disappointing encounters. She'd been bruised from having fended off another thoughtless grope, a typically suggestive innuendo. She'd been dealing with them since she hit puberty, and the one man who she'd actually let breach her defences… well, she wasn't going to think about him. But for her, marrying someone for the sheer convenience of it had seemed like a no-brainer.

But as for Christos…? She hadn't ever truly understood why he'd shown up at her office the next day, with the terms of the marriage outlined in boldfaced type, ready to go over every detail. Seeming enthused about the whole idea, and as reassuringly pragmatic as she'd been. She'd pressed him on the point, and the only information he'd given her was that he preferred to avoid messy emotions, something she could certainly get on board with. And so she'd agreed to it all with alacrity, pushing aside the unease she'd had about why *he* was willing to agree to a marriage made on paper.

And yet…was it really just about fending off would-be Mrs Diakoses? What else could it be? She'd never truly known, but she'd put a prenup in place just in case, even though he made twenty times the amount she did, and she made sure, as ever, to guard her heart, which was far more precious than anything in the bank.

'So, are you going to elaborate on this particular proposal?' Christos asked after a moment, his voice still as relaxed as his stance. 'Because I assume there's a little more to it than what you just said.'

'Yes, there is.' She glanced around the room in all its bland, businesslike impersonality, wishing they were somewhere a little more comfortable. A little *friendlier*, because it was hard enough to go over the practicalities of baby-making while standing in such a sterile room, although maybe she should take advantage of the whiteboard to outline her points.

Number one...you don't need to be involved beyond the obvious.

Christos, as he so often did, immediately picked up on what she was thinking about the room. 'This seems like the sort of discussion we need to have somewhere more comfortable,' he remarked, sliding his phone out of his pocket.

'What are you doing?' she asked as he thumbed a text.

'I have the penthouse suite here on standby,' he explained with a shrug. 'We can go there to talk.'

'Oh, do you?' She couldn't quite keep the telltale sharpness from her voice. Part of their arrangement had been they were free to conduct affairs with other people, as long as they were completely, utterly discreet, but she found she didn't really need or want the reminder right now.

He looked up from his phone, his expression a cross between wry and exasperated. 'For business meetings, Lana. Or VIP clients. Not my...perceived paramours.'

'I don't care about your paramours,' she tossed back at him, and he slid his phone into his pocket.

'I know. I can pick up the key card for the penthouse at Reception.'

Already he was striding forward, sliding his arm under hers, his long fingers resting on her bare wrist, making her pulse jump. Did she really want to go to the penthouse suite with him? In the three years of their marriage, he'd never made a single physical advance, not even a potential innuendo or suggestive remark, and she'd been both glad and grateful. He'd been the perfect gentleman for the entire time, and there was no reason to think he'd change now, simply because she'd told him she wanted his baby.

Right?

'I'm presuming,' he remarked dryly as he guided her towards the lobby, 'that this is just an initial discussion, not a potential act of consummation?'

Lana nearly choked. 'Of *course*—'

'I just wanted to reassure you,' he cut across her, 'because you were looking kind of nervous.'

'I'm—'

'And,' he added imperturbably, 'to tell you the truth, I'm not really in the mood right now. It's been a tough week.' He grinned wickedly at her then, a gleam of teeth and glint of eye that belied what he'd just said and made her body spark to life—again.

She'd always known Christos had a keen sense of humour, but she hadn't quite seen—or felt—it like this before, with such a dangerous, exciting edge that ran like a razor along her nerve endings, twanging everything to life. The last thing she needed right now was to feel the zing of attraction for such an impossible man, and yet…

'Good to hear,' she managed, hoping her voice sounded as light as his did. 'Because I'm not in the mood, either.' Frankly, she never was. Not any more. Even if feeling Christos's arm twined with hers was making her achingly aware of him—his body, his heat, his scent.

A few seconds later he'd accepted the key card from the member of staff at the reception desk, and then they were soaring upwards in the penthouse's private lift, towards the sky.

'I've never been in the penthouse of this particular hotel,' Lana remarked as the doors opened to a large living room, all black marble and scattered leather sofas, with floor-to-ceiling windows overlooking Manhattan's glittering skyline on three sides, Central Park a swathe of darkness in the middle.

'I find one penthouse is much like any other,' Christos replied carelessly, tossing the key card onto an ebony console by the elevator as he strolled into the soaring space. 'You really just get them for the view.'

Lana walked to the window, nerves still racing through her body. She'd got this far, she told herself, and at least Christos was interested in what she had to say. 'It is quite a view,' she remarked, nodding towards the lights of the city.

'Yes, it is.' He spoke from right behind her, his breath warm on the nape of her neck, and she jumped a little, whirling around as she let out an unsteady laugh. 'You surprised me,' she said, one hand pressed to her chest.

'I know.' He eyed her thoughtfully, rocking back on his heels, his hands shoved into the pockets of his trousers. 'And you surprised me. Of all the proposals to suggest…what do you mean, Lana, you want my baby?'

Lana tried not to cringe—I want your baby. It sounded like a tabloid headline. Why had she said it like that? And yet it was true, and he'd cut to the chase as always, with no prevarication or pretence. She struggled to know how to answer, to explain. They'd always promised to be honest with one another, the only way their sort of marriage could work. She didn't want to lie now, far from it, but she still felt she had to handle the truth carefully. There was simply too much at stake not to.

'I want a baby,' she stated baldly. 'A child of my own.'

Something flickered in his eyes. 'And my own, presumably.'

'Well, that part seemed to make sense.' She moved past him, towards the trio of sofas scattered across the black marble floor, resisting the urge to wipe her suddenly damp palms on the satin material of her haute couture dress. She had thought through this. At least, she believed she had, although now that she was saying it all out loud, she wasn't quite as sure. But she'd had to do something, after hearing the news. She'd been galvanised into action… but had she been precipitous? 'Considering we're already married,' she explained over her shoulder.

'One of the tenets of our marriage was no children,' Christos reminded her. He shrugged out of his suit jacket, tossing it on a chair before he joined her by the sofas, sitting down in the middle of the one opposite, arms stretched across the back, the cotton stretching across his powerful shoulders and lean yet muscular chest, the epitome of relaxed power.

Lana curled up in the corner of another, kicking off her heels and hiking her dress up around her calves. She couldn't keep from letting out a sigh of relief to have the designer stilettos off her feet.

'Why do you wear those again?' Christos asked, cocking an eyebrow towards the shoes in question.

Lana shrugged. 'They're a power move.'

'And you're all about those,' he acknowledged wryly, while she nodded back. Yes, she was. Projecting power, being confident, never being taken advantage of—or hurt—again. 'So how does a child fit into your business plan, Lana?' Christos asked. 'Because as I recall, that was why you didn't want children. You were admirably career focused.'

'I still am, but I've reached a point in my career where I can afford to hand projects to some trusted deputies,' Lana replied. She'd thought that part through carefully in these last three days. 'If I had a baby, I'd take three months' maternity leave to start, and then go back part-time for another nine months. After that I'd have to see what was best for both the baby and me.' She wasn't going to have a child just to hand it over to a nanny, not completely, anyway, but neither was she going to completely sacrifice her career. She'd find a balance.

'I see,' Christos replied slowly. His gaze was moving over her again, in thoughtful study, yet revealing nothing. 'So why the change of heart about motherhood?'

Lana hesitated. She needed to be honest, yes, she wanted to be, but she also hated showing weakness. Being vulnerable in any way at all—physically, emotionally, either…both.

'Lana,' Christos said softly, and she knew what he was thinking. *Be honest.* He'd felt her hesitation, had understood what it meant. What else did he understand about her? It was something she wasn't prepared to think about, at least not now.

'I had a doctor's appointment,' she admitted reluctantly. 'And it turns out I'm in the beginning stages of early menopause.'

'Menopause.' Christos looked shocked, that sleepy, thoughtful look dropping away instantly. 'But you're only thirty-two.'

She shrugged, trying to act as if she'd accepted the news when it still felt blisteringly raw. 'One per cent of women experience menopause before forty. I'm one of the unlucky ones, it seems.'

His mouth turned down at the corners, green eyes

drooping in sadness as he leaned forward. 'I'm sorry, Lana.' His tone was low and heartfelt. She knew he meant it.

'Thank you.' She drew a breath that hitched revealingly. She hated him knowing almost as much as she hated having it be true. Yes, she'd said she hadn't wanted children—mainly because she hadn't trusted herself as a mother. It wasn't as if she'd had a good example, after all, but claiming her career had been an easy out, so she hadn't had to get into the mess of her childhood—a single mother who had blamed her for her dad's desertion, always resentful, angry, bitter, mean. Lana had grown up learning to brace for the emotional and physical blows, and she'd moved on at just seventeen, working her way through college, living in a series of awful apartment shares, working hard, desperate to prove herself—and to be loved.

So, so desperate. Thankfully she'd moved past that, but now she was going to have to convince Christos she really did want to have a baby, be a mother. 'It was a shock, I can tell you,' she admitted, hearing the slight thickening of her voice before she managed to get herself under control. 'It's true that I always thought I didn't want kids, but I also thought I had all the time in the world to decide for sure. It turns out I didn't. Don't.'

'And so, time is of the essence with this plan of yours,' Christos surmised quietly. He leaned back again, arms folded.

'Well—yes.' She glanced at him from under her

lashes, feeling uncertain. He seemed to be taking this all in his stride, but how did he really feel about it? She hadn't even explained what she actually meant yet. Maybe she should do that now. 'But I want you to know,' she told him stiltedly, 'that this wouldn't actually affect you in any way.'

Although he'd been completely still, it felt as if he'd gone even stiller. 'It won't? Because having a child generally does, you know.'

'Yes, but…you wouldn't have to be involved. At all.' His expression didn't change, not even a muscle twitching, and Lana rushed on to explain, to reassure. 'Nothing about our agreement, our arrangement, would have to change. I'd have the baby by IVF, and you could be completely uninvolved in its—his or her—upbringing. If you didn't want our—our baby to know you were the father, I'd accept that. I mean, naturally, there might be questions later on, so we'd have to figure how to handle that at some point, but, you know, I'd absolutely respect your privacy.'

She gave a little gulp, wishing he'd say something. Show something. His expression was utterly blank, his body completely still. Wasn't this what he wanted to hear? It was the way her dad had been, the way Anthony had been, not that she'd fallen pregnant with him, but he'd made it *very* clear that if she did, he was not interested. Lana knew, intellectually at least, that Christos wasn't anything like Anthony, but since he'd agreed to the no-children clause, had seemed reassured by it even, surely he would consider this good news? 'Christos?' she prompted uncertainly. 'How does that sound?'

How did that sound? Like the most insulting, unbelievable, *absurd* thing he'd ever heard in his entire life.

Christos stretched his arms back along the sofa, taking a moment to keep his expression relaxed, interested. He wasn't ready yet to show the fury—the *hurt*—he felt. He watched as Lana tucked her hair behind her ears, swallowing several times, clearly nervous—and she was someone who was never nervous. She must realise how badly she'd just insulted him, and on so many levels he couldn't even count them. She was asking him, her *husband*, to be an anonymous sperm donor for the child she'd raise on her own, no help needed or wanted. *As if.* As if he would ever let himself be reduced to that, let *her* reduce him to that, a stud for her own convenience.

'Can you expound on some of the particulars?' he asked mildly, and, to both his annoyance and amusement, he saw she looked relieved by the question. As if a few details were going to change his mind, reassure him. Still, he wanted to know what she was thinking, how deeply she'd dived down this rabbit hole of hers.

'Yes, of course.' She smiled, or tried to, but he understood the source of at least some of her strain. Early menopause, and at only thirty-two. Even for a woman who had stated she never intended to have children, it had to be a terrible blow. He thought of his own mother, his three sisters, the big, boisterous family he'd always loved, at least until the heart had been ripped out of it, and he'd chosen to walk away—although it had never truly been a choice. How could he have possibly stayed, considering what he'd done, and more importantly what he hadn't? A failure that reverberated through him all these years later and had been part of the reason why he didn't think he wanted children of his own. They were just little people you could mess up, and yet…

Lana wanted his baby. *His baby.* Those words, that knowledge, *did* something to him.

Having her tell him point-blank she wanted his baby had created a sudden, surprising, seismic shift inside him. He'd been fine with the no-child clause because he'd assumed, on a fundamental level, that he couldn't be a good father. He wouldn't be emotionally available; he couldn't let himself care about someone that much. And then Lana had said she wanted his baby, and something in him had crumbled—or maybe exploded. His first thought had been, quite simply, Yes. Yes, he wanted this. He wanted a child. A family. A second chance, a do-over for all the mistakes he'd made with his own family. He was wiser now; he could handle it, he wouldn't let their baby down the way he had his mother, his sister. And he wouldn't do the dangerous thing of falling in love with Lana.

It was perfect. At least, it could be.

'What,' she asked tentatively, 'do you want to know, exactly?'

'Well, everything, really,' he replied in the same easy voice, although keeping that light tone was taking more effort. Part of him wanted to grab her by the shoulders and demand what on *earth* she was thinking, to suggest something so—so *offensive*. Or did she not even realise it was? Could she be that oblivious, that ridiculous? 'How do you envisage this all working?' he asked.

Again, that look of relief, a gleam of confidence in her eyes and she straightened in her seat. 'Well, it's simple, really,' she said.

The tone she took was one he imagined her using in a business meeting, when she told one of her eager clients how she was going to polish his tarnished image, turn him into someone new and shinily improved, his company into *Fortune 500* material.

'What we're going to do is this…'

No. Way. Not this time. Not with him.

'Yes?' he prompted, his tone scrupulously polite.

'Um…yes, sorry.' She gave a little laugh as she shook her head, tucking a strand of strawberry-blonde hair behind her ear. 'Sorry, I didn't expect you to agree to it quite so quickly.'

'I haven't actually agreed,' he pointed out. 'I just want to hear the details.'

A faint blush touched her porcelain cheeks. 'Yes, of course. Well, like I said, I'd want to go with IVF. According to the consultant, my condition has been caught early enough that I should have a fairly good chance of getting pregnant if I can within the next three months or so.'

'Three months,' he mused, nodding. A relatively short window. 'Go on.'

'Since I have no other, um, fertility issues, IVF has a better chance of being successful.'

'Presumably,' Christos remarked after a moment, 'you'd have an even better chance of getting pregnant the old-fashioned way.'

'Well, yes, I suppose, technically.' Once more a faint blush touched her cheeks with pink, reminding him of a sunrise. 'But obviously that's not something we want to—to consider.'

'Obviously,' he agreed, dryly. When Lana had first proposed their paper marriage, she'd made it very clear, *very* clear, that sex would never be part of their deal.

'I just find it complicates things,' she'd said bluntly, without any emotion, her gaze unflinchingly direct, so much so that he'd wondered what experience she'd had to feel so firm about the subject. 'And there's no need to complicate what is meant to be a very simple solution.' Then she'd suggested he have affairs, as long as they were discreet. At the time, bemused but not entirely opposed since they were both being so open-minded, Christos had chosen to be amenable.

He'd been tired of the rigamarole of relationships, of women expecting things he simply didn't have it in him to give. Every time he'd told a woman he would never love her, marry her, or even see her for a fourth date, she'd chosen to see it as some sort of challenge. But not Lana, not in the least. At the time, the novelty had been refreshing, liberating. Three years on, it wasn't quite so much any more; he was starting to realise he wanted more. How much more, he couldn't yet decide, but he knew it was something. Maybe even this—a child. A family.

'So, IVF,' he resumed as Lana gazed at him, seeming torn between uncertainty and hope. 'And that part for me is, I presume, pretty self-explanatory? Self-induced, as it were?'

Her blush deepened but her chin tilted upwards to that determined notch. 'Yes, that's how it's usually done with IVF.'

'I see.' He was afraid he saw all too clearly. She wanted his sperm in a test tube, and that was it. And what did he get in return? Absolutely nothing.

'And after the baby's born?' he inquired politely. It was difficult now to keep an edge from his voice but he thought he just about managed it. 'No involvement then, either, by the sounds of it? This baby of ours won't know I'm his or her father, you said?'

'Not if you don't want them to.'

He let a pause settle between them for just a few seconds. 'And if I did?'

She hesitated, and he could tell by the confusion that crossed her face she hadn't thought this part through clearly, or even at all. She'd assumed he wouldn't. 'Well…of course, I mean, that would be… that would be…acceptable, I suppose.'

Acceptable, if only just? *Maybe?* What an insult. A surge of rage fired through him, and Christos tamped it down. He wasn't going to get angry. Not yet. 'And if I wanted to be involved?' he asked. 'As this child's father? What then?'

Lana looked so surprised, he almost laughed. It was as if such a thought had never even crossed her mind. What, he wondered, had ever given her the impression that he would be a willing sperm donor but an absent father? He might have agreed to her no-child clause, but did she really think he was that sort of man? Three years they'd been together, in a manner of speaking anyway, and she didn't have the first clue about who he was as a person. As a man.

'Well, I…' She licked her lips, shifting in her seat, her long, golden legs revealed as the slit in her dress climbed higher.

Christos yanked his gaze away, kept it on her face. 'Yes?' he prompted.

'I didn't think you would,' she admitted. 'You said before that you never wanted children, when we first agreed to the marriage. You made it very clear that children weren't part of your life plan.'

Had he stated it as baldly as that? Probably. He'd known what it was like to love and lose, to be part of a family that was ripped apart and never truly healed, scars running through its centre for ever. He'd never wanted to open himself up to that kind of pain, that kind of loss, and, moreover, he'd never wanted to have the occasion or opportunity to inflict it, unknowingly, or unwillingly even, unable to keep himself from it, just as he had before.

At least, he'd never thought he wanted those things…until now. Now, when he realised he did, and he was, to his own surprise, willing to risk it… for a child. A father's love—and a child's in return—could be a simple thing. A beautiful thing.

'You're right,' he told her, stretching out his legs in front of him and folding his arms. 'I did say that about not wanting to have children. But obviously you've changed your mind, and maybe I've changed mine.'

Her eyes widened, turning a deeper blue shot through with gold as her gaze blazed into his. 'Have you?' she asked, and he shrugged, nonchalant.

'I must admit, it's an intriguing proposition, what you've suggested. I'm more interested than I might have expected myself to be, as it happens.'

Again with that damned relief, passing over her face in a wave. 'I'm glad you think so. As for your… future involvement, I'm sure we could figure that out in time, some kind of arrangement we both were… comfortable with.'

And what, he wondered sourly, would that be? Every other weekend? A monthly get-together? Christmases and birthdays? Considering he hadn't seen his family in well over a year, and that by choice, his determination to be so involved was a little ironic, if not downright hypocritical. And yet he felt it all the same. Utterly. This was a second chance, a fresh start, and he *wanted* it. 'It's not the sort of thing I'd like to leave to chance,' he told her evenly, and she stilled.

'Not to chance…?'

'Generally speaking, the mother's rights tend to

trump the father's in situations involving custody and the like.' It was a general observation more than anything else, but the last thing Christos wanted was some heated battle over their baby. He would never want to subject a child of his to that.

'Custody...' She sounded shocked as she shook her head. 'Christos, it wouldn't ever come to that.'

'Is that a promise you can make? On *paper*?' The edge was coming through his voice now, like a stain bleeding into cloth, and Lana noticed.

'Christos…' She shook her head again, now more confused than surprised. 'What exactly are you saying?'

She'd been honest, brutally so, and so, he decided, would he. He leaned forward, his relaxed pose shucked like an old skin, revealing the tension and even the fury pulsating underneath. 'What I'm saying,' he told her, his tone turning soft yet lethal, 'is that there is no way I'd ever consider your absurd, offensive, *hare-brained* proposal. No way in hell.'

CHAPTER THREE

LANA HAD NEVER seen Christos angry. It was this realisation that filtered through her stunned brain first as she stared at him uncomprehendingly, taking in his glittering eyes, the colour that slashed his high, bladed cheekbones, the breaths that came too fast. *What...?* What had just happened?

She realised she had to reframe their entire conversation, and it left her feeling as if she'd been knocked, not just off balance, but flat on her face. She, who excelled at other people's public relations, at presenting their new image and predicting the public's response to it, had just failed utterly with her own PR. She'd presented her case badly, and misread Christos's response and intention, as well.

How had she misjudged it all so horrendously? Because it *was* horrendous, to see him looking so furious with her. She realised she'd taken his benevolence for granted, because she'd always known him to be kind, thoughtful, considerate. They'd shared a certain trust as well as affection, and she'd liked it. She'd trusted it.

But right now, he looked positively enraged, and she felt something in her shut down, the way it had when her mother had used to turn on her as a child, that dangerous glitter in her eyes, or Anthony had frozen her out, ignoring her in public while she tried not to beg and did anyway.

She wouldn't be like that now, yet she knew she didn't have the strength of will to lighten the mood, to offer a wry remark. *Don't sugar-coat it, darling.* The words floated up to the surface of her brain, but she couldn't say them. She simply stared at him, and he stared back, his fury cooling into something icy and hard.

'I didn't mean to make you angry,' she finally said, her tone quiet but firm. She wouldn't back down, not the way she used to, cowering and cringing to her mother, pleading with Anthony. No. She'd never be that person again.

'Yes, I'm aware of that.' He leaned back again, in the same relaxed pose, yet every muscle was taut, tense, his whole body bristling with restrained energy. 'I'm not sure if that makes it better or worse, to be honest.' His tone almost managed to be wry, but still held an edge. 'Why did you think I would be amenable to such an idea, Lana? I know I said I was okay with not having children, but to donate my sperm for a baby I won't even be bringing up? From a purely selfish point of view, what would be in it for me?'

Realisation hollowed her stomach out. 'Nothing,' she admitted after a moment. Why had she not considered that angle before? Of course Christos wanted something from the deal—but what? 'Although I'm not sure what was in our marriage, for you, besides getting some grasping women off your back. Not much of an incentive, really, as far as I could see.'

His expression turned both thoughtful and guarded, like a veil dropping over his eyes. 'Obviously it was enough of an incentive for me to agree to it,' he replied. 'And don't underestimate the convenience of not being besieged by grasping women. But *this*…if I didn't want a child in the first place, I'd hardly be amenable to donating my sperm to my own *wife*. And if I did want a child, I'd want to be involved. Don't you think?'

Misery swamped her and she had to bite her lip to keep from showing how devastated she felt. When he pointed it out like that, it was obvious, unbearably so. She'd been so *stupid*, because she'd been blinded by her own need and fear. Hearing the doctor tell her that her time was running out…realising this would be her only chance at a child, a family… The family she'd never thought she'd dare to have, a baby to love… She'd let that emotion guide her, and not the cool, clear logic that usually did. Head over heart every time, wasn't that her hard and fast rule? Not this time, though. Not when it had mattered the most.

'I mean, why me?' Christos continued, his tone affable yet relentless. 'If you just want a sperm donor, why not just get a sperm donor?'

Another fair and somewhat obvious point. What could she say? The truth, she supposed. She'd been honest so far, and she'd continue to be so, even if it hurt. 'I trust you,' she told him. 'And I… I like you. And…you have good genes.'

'Your three points regarding the conception of our child,' Christos filled in dryly.

Lana gave a soft huff of laughter. Trust Christos to make a joke about it. She liked that about him, too. 'And point four, you have a good sense of humour,' she quipped before adding, 'I suppose I didn't think this through as much as I should have.' She rolled her eyes, trying to laugh at herself, at least a little, even though she still felt as if she were reeling. 'The truth is, I got the news about my—my condition, and I raced to find a solution. And this one seemed…obvious, I suppose. I didn't mean to offend you. I genuinely believed you wouldn't want to be involved, based on what you've said earlier.'

Something flashed across his face, and she realised she'd hurt him with that admission. What kind of man would refuse involvement with his own child? And yet her own father had, and easily so, according to her mother. She'd assumed Christos would be the same without ever thinking it through. Without thinking about what it would say about him, when she realised now that he would never have been like that. 'Obviously, that wasn't a fair assumption to make,' she offered quietly. 'I'm truly sorry.'

He gave a rather terse nod, his jaw still tight. 'Apology accepted.'

She'd made a mess of things, Lana realised, and she hadn't even got what she wanted out of it. A sigh escaped her before she forced herself to rally. To be practical, because that was what she did. There was still a solution to be found here, and that was what she had to focus on. 'Well, if I did go the sperm donor route,' she asked him, 'how would you feel about that? Assuming we remain married, people will no doubt think the baby is yours.'

'They'd have thought that when you were proposing this baby *would* be mine,' Christos pointed out. 'And you still didn't want me involved.'

'It wasn't a question of want—'

'Wasn't it?' he interjected, and now he sounded unexpectedly weary. 'Trust me, Lana, I think I know you pretty well, after three years. You like to be in charge, calling all the shots.'

'Doesn't everyone?' she returned, her tone turning defensive. He talked about it as if it were a bad thing, but who didn't want to be in control of their own life? She knew what it was like *not* to be in control, to let other people call the shots. Of course she was glad she had more agency now.

'The thing with a baby,' he told her, leaning forward a little, 'is it usually involves two parents. Two people calling the shots. Making compromises, working together.'

Briefly she thought of her mother, the bitterness etched on her face for ever, the father who had walked out when she was just six months old, without a single backward glance, never in contact again. 'Not always,' she told Christos quietly.

He knew she'd been raised by a single mother;

back when they'd first hammered out the details of their marriage, they'd given each other potted histories of their childhoods. She'd told him how her dad had abandoned her and her mother; he'd disclosed that his mother had died when he was sixteen. Neither of them had either asked for or given further details, and Lana had always supposed the lack of knowledge, of understanding, suited them both fine, although admittedly sometimes she had wondered, wanted to know more.

Now he acknowledged her point with a nod. 'But I'm sure you can agree,' he continued smoothly, 'that it's generally better for a child to be raised by two loving parents.'

'If it's possible,' Lana replied, feeling hesitant even though she did technically agree with what he was saying. She had the feeling she was about to be bounced into something, and she wasn't sure what it was. Christos's expression had turned intent, a small, knowing smile flirting with his lips. If only she knew what he was thinking, but the truth was, she didn't. Despite three years of marriage, she *didn't* know him pretty well. That, it seemed, was where they differed.

'So, when it is possible, it's the ideal?' he surmised, eyebrows raised, attitude expectant. 'The thing to aim for, the gold standard?'

She gave a little shrug, a bit impatient now, edgy, wanting him simply to spit out whatever it was he had to say. 'Yes, the ideal, the ultimate, the paragon, the *epitome* of happy families,' she replied, rolling her eyes again. '*Yes*, fine. What of it?'

'Then why would you mess around with a sperm donor and IVF and all that rigmarole,' Christos returned, 'when you have the ideal, the ultimate, the paragon, the *epitome*, sitting right here?'

She blinked at him. Blinked again. What, exactly, was he trying to say?

'Me, Lana,' he explained, and now she heard the humour in his voice again, and she felt as if something in her had settled, righted. This was the man she knew. Trusted. Liked.

'You.' She raised her eyebrows, smiled a little. She wasn't flirting, absolutely not, but…she liked having him back the way he normally was—funny, wry, affectionate, unthreatening. It made something spark inside her, turn fizzy…although she still hadn't completely cottoned on to what he was suggesting.

'Yes. Me,' he reiterated. 'And you. Having a baby—and a family—the old-fashioned way.'

It genuinely hadn't crossed her mind. Christos could see that right off. The way her eyes widened with shock and her expression turned dazed, her lips parting slightly as she simply stared at him.

'You aren't serious,' she finally said, her voice little more than a whisper.

Christos would have been offended, except he knew Lana too well for that. Attraction wasn't the problem here. He'd always felt it from her, like a live wire they had both made sure never to touch. Lana might not yet have admitted it to herself, but it was there. He wasn't wrong about that.

As for him…well, that definitely wasn't a problem, either. It never had been. Even when he'd agreed to the no-sex rule, he'd known he was attracted to her. He'd even wondered if one day Lana might change her mind, and he'd known, right from the beginning, that he would always be amenable…as well as patient. But now?

'I am absolutely serious,' he told her. 'We're married. You want a baby. It turns out I might, too, somewhat to my surprise, it's true. Why wouldn't we do it the way people have been doing it for millennia?'

'Because…' She shook her head, her eyes flashing with both humour and ire. 'That is far more complicated than what I was suggesting!'

'Is it?' he challenged levelly. 'Really? When Junior asks where Daddy is, you didn't think that was going to be a little complicated? Or when everyone assumes he or she is my baby, and they're *right*, but somehow you haven't mentioned it to the person to whom it matters most, our baby? Lana, that's the *definition* of complicated.'

A blush touched her cheeks again, and she looked down, a strand of strawberry-blonde hair falling against her cheek. 'All right, I may not have thought *every* implication through,' she admitted. 'But getting that…involved…feels complicated to me. Very complicated.'

He studied her for a moment. 'Surely sex is preferable to the IVF route, with all the injections of hormones, the emotional upheaval, the palaver, the uncertainty. From what I've heard about it, and admittedly that's not that much, it sounds pretty difficult.'

Her blush deepened and she kept looking at her lap. In three years, he'd never mentioned the S-word to her. She'd taken it so definitively off the table in their original discussion, and with her reasons being about men forever trying to take advantage of her, he'd felt strongly that he needed to show her he wasn't the same.

And so, for three years his gaze had never strayed below her admittedly lovely face. He'd never made a single suggestive remark. Never touched her except on her arm or occasionally put his own around her shoulders, when they were in company, simply as a gesture of togetherness, solidarity. They'd never even kissed, in all this time, and yet he had no doubts she was attracted to him. Just as he was to her. He felt it like a current in the air, a spark leaping between them, and one he looked forward to fanning into flame.

'Maybe it would be less complicated in the moment,' she finally replied, and it took him a second to recall what she was talking about—sex. Specifically, them having it. 'But in the long term… I don't know.'

'What's making you so uncertain?'

She finally looked up, and her expression was composed, even a little resigned. 'The whole point of our marriage was to simplify things. To not involve emotions or—the physical side. To keep it…transactional.'

'Has it really just been transactional?' Christos countered. He knew he was skating on thin ice by simply asking the question, but he was willing to risk it…for now. 'We've been friends, of a kind, haven't we, Lana? Over the years?' He'd like to think they had. They'd certainly enjoyed a camaraderie, of sorts, when their paths had crossed, at least. He enjoyed her company, and he was pretty sure she enjoyed his. They had interesting discussions; they made each other laugh. That, to him, was a pretty strong basis for a marriage…and a family. The family he knew he now wanted.

She looked startled, but then she smiled, her features softening, suffused with genuine warmth. When she looked like that…well, it was a kick to the gut. As well as to another region. 'Yes,' she agreed, her voice as warm as her expression. 'We're friends, Christos.'

'So, we can stay friends.' He made it sound simple, because it was, wasn't it? At least, it could be. As first she'd spoken, and then he had, it had become clearer in his mind. Their marriage of convenience had had its benefits. Their baby of convenience could, too. It really could be that easy. 'A marriage made on paper,' he clarified, 'with a pregnancy clause.'

She let out a startled laugh. 'That's some merger.'

The smile he gave her was certain rather than suggestive, even as his blood heated and his mind raced with provocative images he did his best to banish—for now. 'Exactly.'

'Christos...' She was blushing again, shaking her head, shifting in her seat, responding to him in a way he loved to see. 'Yes, we're friends,' she stated. 'But I told you before that sex complicates things, and I still believe that. Emotions become involved. Feelings get hurt.'

'Yes, when there are certain expectations,' he agreed, even as he wondered when that had happened to her. Her romantic history was completely unknown to him, but he'd certainly been on the wrong side of that bargain himself, in the past. 'But we know what we do and don't want with this, Lana. We want friendship. Companionship. And frankly, the physical side of things would not go amiss, as far as I'm concerned.'

'I doubt you've been missing that,' she returned dryly. 'With your penthouse suite on standby.'

Little did she know. He'd enlighten her at some point, but he wasn't about to freak her out with that information now. 'I mean it.'

She drew a quick, steadying breath. 'All right, so let me hear your proposal. Three points regarding...?' She trailed off expectantly, eyebrows raised, lips pursed.

Christos met her hesitant gaze with a certain one of his own. He might not have worked out all the details or scoured the fine print, but he was sure about this. About them. 'Here they are,' he told her. 'One, we try for a baby the usual way. Two, we raise him or her together. Three, we stay friends and keep love and all its entanglements out of it. For ever.'

Her lips parted and for a second she didn't speak. 'Can it be that easy?' she finally wondered out loud, sounding almost hopeful.

'It can be if we want it to be,' he replied firmly. He truly believed it. 'You haven't fallen in love with me for the last three years, and I haven't fallen in love with you.' Even if sometimes he'd wondered if he *could*. The glossy, iron-willed woman he'd come to know was someone he respected and admired, but not someone, he'd felt, he could ever love…but was that all there was to Lana? He'd sensed something tender underneath, but he'd never tried to probe those depths…and he wouldn't now. Just like Lana, he wasn't interested in loving anyone, except their baby. A parent's love for their child…that felt simple. Easy. Right.

'That might be, but it's not as if we've spent a ton of time together,' Lana protested, which was true enough. They'd kept separate houses throughout their marriage, although they had guest rooms in each other's homes, which they used on occasion. They appeared together frequently enough not to raise eyebrows or make people wonder—more in the beginning, less so three years on. But they'd never really hung out all that much, or shared real confidences, or spent more than an afternoon, maybe an evening, in each other's presence.

'That's true,' Christos acknowledged, 'but don't

you think you would have fallen in love with me already, if you were going to?'

She let out a reluctant laugh. 'Maybe.'

All right, he wasn't going to let that one hurt. It wasn't as if he wanted Lana to fall in love with him. Quite the opposite.

'I don't understand why you suddenly want a baby so much, Christos,' she said quietly. 'When you never did before.'

He shrugged, knowing he would struggle to explain the depth of feeling that had come upon him so suddenly. 'Like you, my biological clock started ticking, I suppose. I didn't realise it until you said something.'

She let out a little laugh. 'Men don't have biological clocks.'

'Now that's just sexist,' he replied, smiling. 'Men can have the desire for children the same way—well, almost the same way—women do. I thought I didn't want to have children because—well, because I didn't want to mess a child up. I still don't.' He smiled wryly, although admitting that much made him feel far too vulnerable. He definitely wasn't going to go any farther with that. 'When you said you wanted my baby, I realised I wanted that, too. I wanted *you* to have my child.'

He let the words linger, so she could absorb the import, the *intent* of them, because he meant every word. Already he was imagining it, in a way he hadn't let himself in three long years. Her body pliant and willing under his, her long, golden limbs splayed and open, handfuls of her sun-kissed hair coursing between his fingers, her lips parted, eyes dazed with desire…

He shut down that line of thought very quickly, before things got out of hand. He shifted in his seat to ease the ache that had started to throb in his groin. Besides, it wasn't just about the sex. He really did want a family. He hadn't expected to want that, hadn't let himself even think about it, not after the disaster he'd made of his own family…but having Lana tell him she wanted a baby had suddenly blown open a door in his mind and heart he'd kept firmly locked for twenty years. A baby of his own, a child they could both love, a family they could create. A new start.

He knew Lana could be coolly pragmatic about most things, but he believed she'd be a good mother. Competent, assured, affectionate, all in, the way she was about everything she cared about. Yes, he was definitely sure about this.

And so, enough with the back and forth, he decided. He'd made his position clear, and frankly he felt it was an offer neither of them should refuse.

'Well, Lana?' he asked, eyebrows raised in gentle challenge. 'What do you say? How about it? Are we going to do this?'

CHAPTER FOUR

LANA STOOD BY the floor-to-ceiling window of her corner office, its view of Rockefeller Plaza beneath her unseeing gaze. She'd paid a fortune for this office, and mainly for the view, but she was blind to it now because all she could think about—all she could see—was Christos Diakos. Her husband.

Well, Lana? What do you say? How about it?

How about *what*? Marriage, in all meaning of the word? Having sex with the man, having a *child* with the man, and yet somehow keeping her head on straight, her heart safe? Last night she'd prevaricated, told him she'd have to think about it for a little while. He'd laughed and said he'd expected no less. He'd risen from the sofa like a man astride the world, totally at ease with himself and the outlandish suggestion he'd just made.

And yet it was what millions of couples embarked on every year. Marriage. Parenthood. Life together, if not love. Why shouldn't she do it? Why did she have to keep herself so apart from everyone?

Because it's what you've learned to do. It's the

way, the only way, you know how to stay safe. To be in control.

But maybe safe was overrated. As for control…

And anyway, Lana reminded herself, she would be safe, heart-wise. Christos had been right. If they were going to fall in love with each other, they would surely have done it already. The fact that they hadn't meant they wouldn't. Right? They'd both been successfully inoculated against the dreaded L-word, at least with each other. And the truth was, she both liked and trusted him; she enjoyed his company—his easy humour, his innate kindness, his unapologetic professional ambition. So why not enjoy all the fringe benefits of such a union—a baby and, more immediately, *making* a baby—and not worry about emotions that wouldn't become engaged?

Could it really be that easy? Did she even want it to be? Sex was still scary to her, after her experience with Anthony, the way he'd pour scorn on her in her most vulnerable and needy state. Did she want to go through that with Christos, even if she knew—at least in her head—that he would be different?

A shuddering breath escaped her. She glanced down at the ground forty floors beneath her and felt as if she were about to take a leap right out there, onto the statue of Atlas in the centre of the plaza, his broad shoulders reminding her of Christos's last night, when he'd been stretched out on that sofa, looking relaxed and powerful, potently male and utterly assured of his own charisma. He hadn't had any doubts that she would want to consummate their marriage, had he? And why should he, when he was a man most in demand—or had been, before his marriage?

What women had slept with him since, she tried to never let herself think about. Jealousy was an emotion she definitely did not intend to feel. But if they did do this the old-fashioned way, then fidelity was a must. Wasn't it? It was one of many details they hadn't discussed yet.

'Lana?' Her assistant and most trusted member of staff, Michelle, came to the doorway of her office. 'You have a call from Bluestone Tech on line two?'

Albert from last night, wanting to refer his awkward friend who needed a rebrand. Lana always welcomed business, although her calendar was completely full for the next six weeks. After that, she might want to clear it completely…a possibility that filled her with fear and excitement in equal measure. Could she even do the motherhood thing, considering the sorry example of her own? She wanted to believe she could, but she struggled with doubts.

'Can you tell him I'll call him back?' Lana asked Michelle, who frowned, glancing around the empty office, before she nodded and retreated back out to the reception area where she had her own desk.

With another gust of breath, Lana walked back to her desk, a single, sculpted piece of walnut, and sat down. She had plenty of work to do—a party to plan, a publicity blitz to launch, calls to return, emails to send, wheels to grease, and yet right now she couldn't focus on anything. Anything but Christos.

She was still staring blankly into space when Michelle came back into her office, armed with a double espresso. 'I thought you needed it,' she said as she set the cup down in front of Lana.

'Thank you.' Lana took a much-needed sip before glancing up at her assistant. 'How did you know?'

'You've been acting distracted all morning, which isn't like you. You've usually ploughed through your inbox twice over by now.' Michelle cocked her head. 'What's up? If you want to tell me, that is?'

Michelle, Lana knew, was the one person she trusted absolutely, more so even than Christos, although that was simply because Christos was a man, and she'd learned never to trust men. From the time she'd hit puberty at age eleven, men had been looking at her, making remarks, innuendos, sometimes even trying to grope or touch her. Whether it was the blonde hair or big boobs Lana didn't know, but something about her physique made men think she welcomed their attention when the exact opposite was true. She'd thought Anthony was different, with the way he'd wined and dined her, but in the end he hadn't been. He'd actually been worse.

Still, she trusted Christos more than she trusted any other man, that was for certain. But Michelle she trusted with the truth. Her assistant knew the truth of her marriage, had even been impressed by Lana's matter-of-factness about it.

'Don't you get lonely, though?' she'd asked when Lana had explained it to her, and Lana had given a short laugh.

'No,' she'd said, which was probably the only time she hadn't been honest with Michelle. Yes, she got lonely, but she'd learned that was far better than the alternative. She'd take loneliness any day over heartbreak, humiliation, hurt. Yes, indeed.

'Christos and I had a discussion,' Lana told Michelle now as she took another sip of coffee. 'We're thinking of having a baby together.'

'What?' Michelle's mouth fell open. 'You want kids?'

'Well, *a* kid, yes.' Lana smiled wryly. 'It turns out I have a biological clock, after all.'

'But what about LS Consultants?' Michelle asked. 'Your life is this place, Lana—'

'I'm not going to walk away from it, don't worry,' Lana assured her. 'But with trusted associates like you, I think I could probably take a couple of months off.'

'Wow.' Michelle shook her head slowly. 'I didn't see that one coming.'

'No?' To be fair, she hadn't seen it coming, either. Not until that doctor's appointment four days ago, when she'd discovered what the night sweats, irritability and irregular periods had really meant—something she still needed to absorb. Accept.

And meanwhile…

'So, what does this mean for you and Christos?' Michelle asked. 'Because this doesn't sound like much of a convenient marriage to me, not any more.'

'Well, it would be, sort of.' Lana gave her assistant a rueful smile. 'We both realised we wanted a family, and it made sense to start one together. But nothing else will change.' Or so she kept telling herself.

Michelle waggled her eyebrows, looking both sceptical and amused. 'I'd say *something* is going to change. Unless you've figured out another way babies come about?'

Lana smiled thinly. She was *not* going to mention the whole IVF debacle to her assistant. Twenty-four hours later and the concept now made her cringe. What *had* she been thinking of, suggesting such a thing? And yet what was Christos thinking of now? Because she was still apprehensive about how it would all actually work. 'All right, maybe that will change,' she allowed. 'But that's just one aspect.'

'Some aspect,' Michelle replied with a grin while Lana tried to get a grip on the panic that was icing her insides. Yes, some aspect, indeed, and one she hadn't considered or engaged in in a *very* long time, for a reason. Not that she particularly wanted Christos knowing that, but…

'So how will it work?' Michelle asked, as if reading Lana's mind. 'Practically, I mean, please don't give me the nitty-gritty.' She held up a hand as she gave a not-so-mock shudder. 'But in terms of your relationship? Will you live together? In whose house? How will you share the parenting responsibilities? Are you going to be a regular married couple now?'

'No, definitely not,' Lana replied to the last question with a firmness she felt absolutely, even if she couldn't yet anchor it in fact. 'We won't love each other, for a start.'

Michelle stared at her, nonplussed. 'What does that even mean?'

'What do you mean, what does it mean?' Lana asked, a bit rattled by the question. 'Wasn't it obvious? It means exactly what it sounds like it means: We. Won't. Love. Each. Other.' Simple, right?

'Ye-es,' Michelle allowed, 'but if you'll be married, living together, parenting together, *sleeping* together...assuming you're doing all this without gritted teeth or bad attitudes...what does it mean you won't love each other? That sounds a lot like love to me, or the facsimile of it, anyway.'

Lana almost laughed at the blithe naiveté of such a question. 'That's not love,' she stated firmly. 'That's friendship. Love is something else entirely.' Love was a sick, hollow feeling at your centre, radiating outward, taking you over. It was a weakness that stole through your body and heart and left you writhing with pain and gasping for air. Love was need, and fear, and disappointment, and shame.

Love was not something she was going to feel for Christos Diakos, or anyone else, ever again. She'd seen her mother grow twisted and bitter, angry and old, all from loving a man. She'd felt her own heart split right in half when the one man she'd dared to give even a *piece* of herself to had walked away without a backward glance, just as her father had. It was what she'd thought all men did...until she'd met Christos.

Could she really trust him—not with her heart, no, never that, but with this much? Her happiness? Her *child*?

'We have some details to work out,' she told Michelle. And she realised she needed to talk to Christos about them asap.

Christos glanced down at the text from Lana on his phone in pleased amusement.

Need to talk details asap.

This was a good sign, he thought as he thumbed a quick text back. A very good sign.

Where and when?

The Metro Club, in twenty?

She'd named the private club for Manhattan's professional elite known for its elegance and discretion, where they occasionally met for a businesslike briefing on the state of their marriage, sharing calendars, planning what events they'd attend together.

He texted back, realising he was smiling.

I'll order you an espresso.

Make it a double.

He let out a little huff of laughter.

Of course.

* * *

Exactly eighteen minutes later, he was seated on a leather sofa in a quiet alcove of the club's lounge overlooking Madison Avenue, sipping his Americano and answering emails on his phone while he waited for Lana to arrive. He felt her presence before he saw her, like an electricity in the air, and he looked up to see her poised in the doorway of the lounge, elegant as ever in an ice-blue silk blouse and form-fitting skirt in navy, her hair swept up into a chignon, a few wisps dancing about her face. She saw him then, and her eyes widened for a second, and it felt as if a jolt passed between them, that live wire twanging to life.

Well, wasn't *that* interesting? For three years they'd managed to exchange glances across crowded rooms and never feel that electric energy, at least no more than a distant pulse of it. Now Christos was sure they both definitely did. Another good sign.

She started walking towards him through the scattered sofas and tables of the lounge, a loose, long-legged stride that made men's heads turn, because she was that beautiful, and not just beautiful, but magnetic. Gazes were drawn, eyes widening in appreciation. Even Christos found he couldn't tear his gaze away. He kept the faint smile on his face as she reached the sofa where he was sitting, dropping her expensive leather bag on the floor before she slid into the leather armchair opposite.

'Thank you for this,' she said as she picked up her

espresso and took a sip, eyes lowered so her golden lashes brushed her pale cheeks.

'Of course.' He waited a beat for her to swallow, and then asked in the same amenable voice he'd been using all along, 'So what details did you want to discuss?'

She put her cup down with a slight clatter and took a deep breath before she looked up at him, her gaze as unflinchingly direct as ever, but with a shadow of…something in it. Something that gave Christos a slight pause, a frisson of unease. He realised he wanted Lana to be the way she normally was—briskly pragmatic, able to laugh at herself, beautiful and funny and smart. Not…*vulnerable*, even just a hint of it lurking in her shadowed gaze, because he really wasn't good at dealing with that.

'I've made a list,' she said, and took her phone out of her bag.

Christos found himself breathing a small sigh of relief. Lists he could do. Lists were what Lana did, and it reassured him. As long as they kept this practical, they'd be fine. He'd be fine. It was when someone said they needed him that he found himself shutting down, walking away. He wished he were different, but he wasn't. He knew that from bitter experience…his mother, his sister. But he wouldn't be like that with Lana, because he wouldn't let himself…and she wouldn't, either. 'All right, tell me what's on it.'

She swiped the screen of her phone a few times and then frowned as she glanced down at her bullet points, her nose wrinkling in a way he'd always found endearing. She had a few golden freckles scattered across her nose that Christos knew she covered with face powder, but when she crinkled her face in thought they always reappeared.

'All right, first point.'

'Are there three?' he interjected, and she looked up, smiling, as she rolled her eyes.

'Three points regarding the details of our union? I suppose I could re-outline.'

'No, just hit me with the first one,' he replied, leaning back. 'I'm ready.'

'Okay.' She took a quick breath. 'Would we share the same house?'

'Yes,' he answered promptly, surprised at just how strongly he felt about that. 'If we have a baby together, we're not going to live separate lives any more. It wouldn't be good for our family.'

'Whose house?'

He shrugged. 'I really don't mind.' He thought of his soaring bachelor loft apartment in Soho, with its retro ironwork and huge skylights, and then her more stately brownstone on the Upper West Side, three stories of carefully curated shabby chic. 'Maybe yours, since it's a bit more family friendly? I don't want Junior to try climbing the spiral stairs to my loft.'

She seemed pleased by that idea, a small, relieved smile curving her lips before she nodded. 'Okay, that makes sense.'

'Next point?' Maybe this would be even easier than he'd thought. Hoped.

She glanced down at her phone. 'After I became pregnant, assuming I did, would we…?' She paused, colouring a little, and Christos filled in, knowing already what she was going to ask.

'Would we continue our state of joyful union?'

Something flashed across her face, a cross, perhaps between amusement and alarm. 'Well, yes.'

He shrugged expansively. 'What would be the reason not to?'

She swallowed. 'I can think of several.'

'Oh?' Now he was curious. 'And what are they?'

'Well, what I said before, about sex complicating things.' She was definitely blushing now, and she put her phone down and reached for her espresso, mainly, Christos thought, to hide behind her cup.

'I thought we dealt with that last night. We haven't fallen in love with each other, and we're not going to.'

'All right, but…' She put her cup down. 'If we were married—'

'We are married,' he reminded her.

'Properly married. Living together, raising a child together, sleeping together… I'd expect… I'd need you to be faithful.' She spoke as if he would find this difficult, as if it might be a deal-breaker for him, to be faithful to his own wife.

Christos stared at her for a moment, wondering what was going on in her mind. What experiences, what *pain*, had led her to think that he would find such a clause unacceptable?

'Which makes us continuing our joyful union all the more essential,' he replied. 'Of course I'd be faithful to you. And I would expect you to be faithful, as well.'

Relief as well as surprise passed across her face in a wave. 'That wouldn't be a problem, trust me.'

Oh, no? How intriguing. Of course, he'd known her attitude towards sex was a little...*cold*, but now he wondered what made it so. Her seeming reticence didn't alarm him. He was a patient man, and he knew, no matter what Lana liked to believe, that she responded to him physically. He'd seen it, felt it—in her hitched breaths, the flush of her face, the way her gaze found his in a crowded room. Yes, she most certainly responded. And he looked forward to having her respond to him even more.

'So, we've covered two points,' he said as he took a sip of his coffee. 'What's number three?'

CHAPTER FIVE

LANA HESITATED, because number three was one she desperately wanted to know the answer to, but it was also the one that made her feel the most vulnerable, the most emotionally exposed, and that was a state of being she tried never to let herself experience. Not any more. She took another sip of her coffee, while Christos waited. Then she put her cup down, and still didn't speak. How to say it? Frame it, without sounding, well, a little pathetic and needy and *sad*?

'Lana?' he prompted.

The gentleness in his voice compelled her to blurt, 'What makes you believe I'd be a good mother?' The compassion that immediately suffused and softened his face made everything in her inwardly squirm. Oh, she hated that look, even as part of her craved it, craved his understanding. And yet she'd never wanted pity, never ever. She wanted to be strong. To *seem* strong, even when she wasn't.

'I just mean,' she hastened to add, 'I'm assuming you think I would be a good mother, or at least an adequate one, since you seem willing to have a child with me.'

'I do think that,' he replied quietly, without any of his usual wryness.

She forced herself to look up at him, even though it hurt a little, because his expression was still soft with sympathy. 'But why do you? I'm asking because I don't think you could actually know, and, frankly, I haven't exactly given off many maternal vibes, have I?' From the beginning of their relationship, she'd made it very clear that she didn't want children, had no interest in them, even. He'd never even seen her hold a baby, because she never had. Why on earth would he think she was mommy material? *Why would she?*

Christos was regarding her steadily, his compassionate look now replaced by a quiet thoughtfulness. Lana made herself hold his gaze, bracing herself for whatever came next.

Actually, Lana, you're right. Now that you've pointed it out, I realise you'd make a pretty crap mother, so maybe we need to rethink this whole idea.

Then, to her surprise, he took her hand in his, his long, lean fingers sliding across hers, sending sparks of awareness shooting all the way up her arm, through her whole body as she tried not to reveal her instant physical reaction. The last thing she wanted right now was to respond to him in that way, and yet the feel of his hand was both comforting and exciting at the same time.

'I think the real question is,' he asked in a low

thrum of a voice that vibrated all the way through her, 'why do *you* think you wouldn't make a good mother?'

Instinctively, without thought, she tried to pull her hand from his, but he tightened his fingers on hers, wrapping around them more securely and holding her in place. The warmth of his palm seeped into her skin, and something even more alarming than those fizzy sparks flooded through her—not just desire, but a deeper emotion, an ache of both longing and acceptance that threatened to undo her completely… all simply from him holding her hand.

This man had the power to affect her...more than she wanted him to. More than he even realised.

She pushed the realisation away, focused on the practicalities. 'I'll be honest,' she told him, glancing down at their twined hands, trying not to feel the warmth of his palm, let it affect her. 'I'm not convinced I will be one, although I'll certainly try my best.'

'I didn't ask that,' Christos replied after a moment. His thumb was now gently stroking her palm, sending shivery bolts of sensation through her, making her feel both sleepy and wide awake at the same time, a yearning unfurling from her centre, radiating outwards, taking her over. Did he realise he was doing it? He must. But why now, when he'd barely touched her in three years?

This was why she'd suggested IVF, Lana thought a little wildly. Because already things had become very, very complicated. For *her*. Not, it seemed, for Christos, and that scared her all the more.

'I didn't ask if,' he told her, 'I asked *why*.'

'I told you why,' Lana replied unsteadily. His thumb was still doing its hypnotising work and she was finding it hard to concentrate. 'Because I haven't ever been maternal. I haven't even *wanted* to be maternal.'

'Why?'

Not another why, for heaven's sake! With what felt like Herculean effort, she managed to pull her hand away from his, but only, she suspected, because he'd let her. She cradled it in her lap, as if it had been injured, hoping he didn't see. 'I told you I grew up with a single mom,' she stated, doing her best to keep her voice brisk. 'Well, *she* wasn't very maternal.' To say the least. 'So, I suppose I never thought I would be.' Had chosen not to be, because she'd seen, she'd felt, how the lack of a mother's love could affect a child. Devastate them emotionally, so they never fully recovered. And she hadn't wanted to take that responsibility, that *risk*, herself with another human being.

Except now, all because of her diagnosis, she was willing to—was she being selfish? What on earth made her think she could actually do it? That she wouldn't mess up her baby's life the way her mom had messed up hers?

Not that she even blamed her mother any more. When her mother had fallen seriously ill five years ago, Lana had forced herself to forgive, to accept, before she had died. It had been important to her to have that reconciliation, and she'd come to realise that her mom had had a very raw deal in life—a husband walking out when she'd had a small baby, a life of hard grind, love affairs with men who had used her and thrown her away. No, Lana no longer blamed her mother for the way she now found herself; she simply accepted it, acknowledged her own weaknesses, tried to work with them.

Maybe this was a bad idea, after all.

'Lana.' Christos's voice was a mixture of stern and gentle. 'Stop freaking out.'

She blinked him back into focus, startled. 'I'm not freaking out.'

'Yes, you are. You're practically hyperventilating.'

To her embarrassment, she realised she was. She'd started breathing faster without even being aware she was doing it. That was what thinking about these kinds of things did to her. She forced herself to let out a long, slow breath and relax in her seat.

'Okay. There.' She managed a smile as Christos cocked his head.

'Do you think you wouldn't love our baby?' he asked, and she sat bolt upright, her breath coming out in something close to a gasp. So much for relaxation.

'Of course I would!'

He leaned back, smiling a little smugly. 'I think so, too. So, so much for not being maternal, eh?'

She shook her head, horrified to find herself near tears. 'It's not that simple, Christos. It's not just about feelings.'

'I didn't say it was simple.'

'You implied it. I can say I'll love my baby. I can even mean it… But will I? When I don't even know what a mother's love looks like?'

He frowned. 'Was your mother that bad?'

Lana thought of her mother's angry rants, the sudden smacks and slaps, the constant, simmering fury and bitterness. 'Well, she wasn't great,' she said carefully. 'She was tired and strung out, and she resented me for being alive and made sure I always knew it. So, it's made me a little wary of loving people, I suppose.'

She was being more honest than she'd ever been with him before and hating it even as she recognised it was necessary, because she *knew* this about herself. She didn't *like* loving people—the utter weakness of it, the endless opening to humiliation and hurt. Would she feel that way with her own child? She didn't want to, she was hoping she'd be different with her baby, but…what if she wasn't?

'I suppose,' Christos replied after a moment, his tone thoughtful, 'that's a risk every mother—every parent—has to take.'

'It's more of a risk for some than others.'

'And you think it's more of a risk for you?' He sounded more curious than alarmed.

'I—I don't know,' she admitted. 'I'm afraid it might be.' She glanced down at her hands, now folded on the table. 'The truth is, I don't—I don't like loving people.'

Christos was silent for a moment. 'And yet you were worried that you might fall in love with me.'

A blaze of shock—as well as an unexpected fury—went through her. 'I never said that!'

He shrugged, unfazed by her ire. 'You implied it, don't you think, when you said sex complicates things? Presumably, that was what you meant.'

Yes, it had been, but she still didn't like him saying it as bluntly as that. She didn't like the way it made her feel, all exposed and raw. 'I'm *not* going to fall in love with you,' she stated fiercely, and he gave her a faint smile.

'Good, because I'm not going to fall in love with you.' Amazing how he could say that as if it was a compliment. He leaned across the table. 'But I think we'll both love our baby, don't you?'

Christos watched as emotions chased across his wife's face—surprise, uncertainty, fear, and then, finally, thankfully, hope.

He sat back as he waited for her to process what he'd said. Admittedly, he was a little shaken, not so much by what she'd said, which he'd sort of guessed the gist of anyway, but with the *way* she'd said it. The vulnerability she'd shown, because he didn't know what to do with it. Just as it always had before, it made something in him start to shut down, a door starting to close, and there was nothing he could do about it but try to act as though it weren't happening.

Briefly, painfully, he let himself think of his mother, Marina Diakos, lying in bed, one scrawny hand outstretched towards him in desperate supplication. *'Christos… Please. I love you.'*

And then his sister, years later. *'Christos, please. Come home. I need you.'*

And he'd walked away from them both.

He forced the memories away. He'd failed his family, he knew he had, because they'd shown him their weaknesses, their need, and he hadn't been able to cope with any of it. He'd rejected them utterly, in a way he could never forgive. But he wasn't going to be that way with Lana, because she wasn't going to need him the way his family had.

So really, he realised uncomfortably, the question she should be asking him wasn't whether she'd make a good mother, but whether he'd make a good father.

He hadn't wanted children before, because he'd been unsure of whether he could be a good father or not. So what made him so confident now, that this could work?

'I certainly hope we'd love our child,' Lana replied, drawing him back to the present. 'Since we want to have one in the first place.'

'There you are, then.' He shrugged away the discomfort of his own thoughts. It *was* simple. At least it could be. They could make it so.

She let out a little sigh. 'Maybe I'm overthinking this, but a baby is a big thing. I don't want to mess it—him or her—up.'

'On that we're agreed.'

She eyed him thoughtfully, her head tilted to one side, a strand of strawberry-blonde hair brushing her cheek. 'You seem so sure about this. So…relaxed.'

He shrugged, wishing he felt as relaxed as he was

acting. Those old memories, those desperate ghosts, had a habit of rising up and reminding him of just how badly he'd let people down. The people who loved him.

But Lana wouldn't love him.

And as for their child…he'd move heaven and earth to be there for his own little boy or girl. He had to hold onto those truths. 'I try to be. I don't know that there's much point in going over all the things that could go wrong.'

'But it's important to be prepared, Christos. Deliberate.'

'I could never accuse you of not being that.' She smiled faintly, and he smiled back, and in that simple exchange, he felt as if something warm and wonderful were exploding in his chest. 'We can do this, Lana,' he told her. He reached for her hands, clasping them in his own. 'Let's not get bogged down in all the what-ifs. We know where we are. We like and respect each other. Neither of us is going to throw a fit or walk away. Why not just…go for it?' And stop thinking so much, because it made him remember, and that made him nervous.

'Even though twenty-four hours ago the prospect of having a baby had never crossed your mind?' she asked wryly.

He couldn't keep from smiling wolfishly back. 'Well, it had crossed my mind. At least, the *how* of it. I can be honest about that.'

For a second her hands tensed in his, and he watched her carefully, wondering how she would react. Even when she'd been talking about him needing to be faithful, they'd somehow skirted around the actual sex part. 'Yes, about the how,' she said, glancing down at their hands.

'Always glad to talk about the how,' he replied lightly, and she looked up.

'According to my doctor, I should be ovulating next week.'

Okay, maybe not *that* kind of how, but fine. He could deal with a conversation about ovulating, no problem. Christos nodded, businesslike. 'So, we'd best get busy?'

'I'll arrange a hotel,' Lana stated firmly, almost as if she'd already made the reservation. 'I think it's best if this—encounter—takes place on neutral territory.'

Neutral territory? 'It's making love, not war,' he quipped, and for a second she looked annoyed, almost angry.

'*Don't* call it that.'

Jeez, she really had a thing about love, but then so did he, so it was fine. 'It's just a phrase, Lana,' he replied mildly. 'All I meant was you sound like you're planning a military manoeuvre.'

'Well,' she said after a second's pause, 'when it comes to this…it feels as if I am.' She glanced at him from under her lashes, clearly gauging his reaction, and the truth was, he wasn't sure how to react. Was she talking about the whole ovulation thing, getting the timings right, or something bigger? Something more fundamental to who she was, what she'd experienced?

Something he couldn't deal with.

'Well, military manoeuvres can be fun,' he told her with another wolfish smile, and after another second's pause, she smiled back, but there was something almost sorrowful in the curve of her lips, the little nod she gave, and he didn't know if she was disappointed in what had amounted to a brush-off, or relieved.

He didn't want to know.

'Well,' she said after a moment, 'I'm sure you have plenty of experience of such *manoeuvres*.'

He tamped down on the flash of irritation he felt at this. Lana had made several of those remarks recently, and he was starting to feel as though she thought he was something of a man whore, when nothing could be further from the truth. Yes, he'd had his fair share of brief liaisons—he'd made no secret of it when they'd first worked out the details of their marriage—but with every woman he'd always made his expectations clear and, in any case, since they'd been married…

Well, he wasn't going into all that just now.

'So, when will this military manoeuvre happen, exactly?' he asked, and, somewhat to his bemusement, she swiped her phone to check her calendar.

'Next week…the fourth or the fifth of June would be best.' Lana kept her lowered gaze on her phone, and he saw her swallow. Gulp, even. 'A week from tomorrow.' She swallowed again, and then, stiffening her spine, put her phone down and looked up. 'Does that suit you?'

'I don't think I have anything on my calendar.' He'd make sure he didn't. 'Does it suit *you*?' he asked, because she did seem to be taking the idea of them having sex quite seriously, and with more than a little trepidation. He thought of her guarded remarks about men over the years, how they'd taken advantage of her.

Never mind whether he'd been discreet about his alleged affairs during their marriage…had she? Had she had them at all? What did she really think—and feel—about sex?

'Yes, it suits me,' she stated firmly. 'That's when I'm ovulating, after all.'

So romantic, but, he supposed, necessary. 'Are you nervous?' he asked, and immediately she looked wary, tucking that strand of hair that had been brushing her cheek behind her ear in a gesture that seemed nervous, no matter how she chose to answer the question.

'No, of course not.' *Of course not?* 'I mean, it's a…development. And it is bound to change things, at least a little.' She managed a smile, humour lighting her eyes briefly. 'You've never seen me naked, for example.'

No, but he was certainly looking forward to that… along with a lot of other things. 'And you've never seen me naked,' he countered. She blushed, which he liked. 'But that, of course, is just the beginning.' The words seemed to hover in the air between them, along with the images they created, at least in his mind, and, he was pretty sure, in her own. Naked bodies, golden and gleaming under candlelight, twisting and writhing with pleasure…

'Right.' The word came out in the manner of a bullet as Lana slapped both hands on the table, bemusing him, as she started to rise. 'I need to get back to work.'

'Fine.' He stood up, reaching for the suit jacket he'd slung over his chair. 'So, have we covered your three points regarding the new status of our marriage? Any further points you wanted to cover?'

'No,' she said after a moment. 'I think that's it.'

'All right, then.' He raised his eyebrows in expectant query. 'Do we need to meet again before D-Day?'

She let out a little laugh. 'I can tell you're going to have fun with the whole military thing.'

'Well, it *is* fertile ground. Literally.'

She rolled her eyes, laughing again. 'All right, fine. Go ahead with the quips. And I don't think we need to meet again. Not until…you know.' She reached for her bag and slung it over her shoulder. 'I'll make the hotel reservation and send you the details.'

'Right.'

She gave a little nod, clearly pleased, clearly thinking she was in control. She'd make the hotel reservation. She'd call the shots. She'd keep everything neat and ordered and under her authority.

Well, maybe not.

'Good. Great.' Another nod while Christos

watched, smiling faintly. 'I know I should have said this before,' she said, 'but…thank you, Christos. You've been more than generous and kind, too, especially considering what I was first suggesting.' She gave a little shake of her head. 'I realise now that the whole IVF thing was a little bit ridiculous, all things considered.'

He raised his eyebrows. 'A little bit?'

'All right, a lot. I just… I suppose I assumed you'd be like all the other men I've known.'

That was an interesting, if sorrowful statement, but one he wasn't about to probe too deeply. 'I look forward to proving otherwise.'

'Thank you.' Another nod. She fiddled with the strap of her bag, and then he saw her professional demeanour come over her like a cloak she drew about herself. Her eyes flashed blue fire and her chin tilted at that determined angle, her lithe body straightening. The only thing she didn't do was click her heels together like a good soldier. 'All right, then,' she said. 'See you next week.'

'See you next week,' Christos echoed as she turned and began to walk out of the club's lounge.

Yes, he thought as he watched her move through the tables and sofas, the admiring glances sent her way, she would see him next week, but not the way she thought she would.

Because if anyone was going to call the shots in their marriage, it was him.

CHAPTER SIX

LANA COULDN'T KEEP a gusty sigh of relief from escaping her as she kicked off her stiletto heels and walked into the living room of her brownstone. She'd had a full day of back-to-back meetings, and her body ached with tension—not from the work meetings, which she'd actually enjoyed, but from the meeting she was going to be having tomorrow night. The *manoeuvre.*

Another sigh escaped her, this one closer to a shudder, and she drew the pins from her hair and shook the tumbled mass down her back as she started to unbutton her blouse. Heading into her bedroom, she shucked off her work outfit and reached for her pyjamas, comfort clothes she never let anyone see her in—old sweats and a T-shirt worn to a paper-thin softness. Her bra went too, tossed into the laundry hamper in the corner. She was going to enjoy this last night of alone time, because tomorrow…

Well, she hadn't actually let herself think that much about tomorrow. She'd made the reservation at one of the city's swankiest hotels, although *not* the penthouse. She'd bought a nightgown, in coffee-coloured silk edged with black lace, not too virginal or romantic or even sexy, but sophisticated, she hoped. She'd booked a morning's worth of spa treatments for tomorrow—waxing pretty much everything, a body wrap, the works. When it came to sex with Christos, she wanted to make sure she was on top form, everything a kind of armour.

Sex with Christos.

A shiver went through Lana, and she thought about how he'd stroked her palm, how she'd responded, that ache opening up inside her. How would she respond when he was touching her far more intimately than that? What if she froze up?

What if she didn't?

It felt like a minefield, and that wasn't even taking into account the emotional side of the whole thing, which clearly didn't bother or even affect Christos, but which she knew she still struggled with. Sex *meant* something to her, which was why she was so scared of having it. Why she hadn't had it in a very, very long time. Should she tell Christos? Prepare him for her own inexperience and inevitable awkwardness? The thought was excruciating.

He viewed sex differently. She knew that. She just had to remind herself from time to time, including now.

Pushing her feet into fluffy slippers—something else she never let anyone see—she headed into the kitchen to make a late dinner. She put a playlist on her phone, hooked up to the surround sound speakers, and the hauntingly melancholy sound of Bach's 'Cello Suite in G Major' floated through the house, one of her favourite pieces of music, for both its sorrow and beauty.

Dinner was a chef-prepped meal she ordered in bulk from a local caterer, something healthy and delicious she could pop in the microwave. As she waited for it to heat, she wondered if she would start cooking when she had a child of her own. Would she make healthy, home-made meals for her family, nurture them with cookies and cakes baked with love?

She wanted to, and yet the thought filled her with something almost like fear. That certainly wasn't how she'd grown up. Did she even know how to do it? She'd never really cooked in all her years; when she'd been young and working her way through college, it had been instant noodles and baked beans. Later, when she'd had the money, it had been meals like this.

But besides the uncertainty about whether she could even manage to make a meal, the thought of her and Christos and their baby seated around a table, bathed in the warm glow of a lamp, eating food she'd made herself…

Well, there was something about that image that terrified her, as well as filled her with a deep and unbearable longing.

She was startled back to reality by the sound of what she thought at first was the microwave dinging, but then realised was actually the chime of the front doorbell. Someone was at her house.

Lana hesitated, caught between wanting to ignore it, in the hope that it was an Amazon delivery, even though she knew she hadn't ordered anything. Her home, three floors of an old brownstone with comfortable furniture in the shabby chic style, was her sacred space, the private sanctuary where she could be safe and alone. She didn't invite people over, and people in Manhattan never just dropped by.

If she ignored it, she thought, whoever it was would probably go away. The microwave dinged, and she opened it and reached for her meal.

The doorbell went again, and then, to her surprise, her phone pinged with a text. Everything, it seemed, was happening at once.

She glanced at her phone, shock icing her insides when she saw it was from Christos.

Open the door. It's me.

What? A ripple of surprise, mixed with both alarm and pleasure, went through her.

She was still staring at the screen when another text appeared.

Seriously, open the door.

What on earth was he doing here? Yes, he'd spent the night sometimes, but in the guest suite on the lower floor, with its own separate basement entrance. And he never came unannounced; that was always one of their rules. Her rules, actually. Visits were always scheduled, because she really didn't do well with these kinds of surprises.

Her phone started ringing.

Warily, Lana swiped to take the call. 'Christos?' she asked cautiously.

'Are you going to open the door?' His voice was rich, velvety, with that hint of humour, and somehow, despite her unease, she found she was smiling.

'How do you even know I'm home?' she asked teasingly.

'I saw you walk up the steps, so that was a clue. Are you going to let me in?'

There was no reason not to, and yet… 'Why didn't you tell me you were coming over?'

'I wanted to surprise you. And we have things to discuss.' His tone managed to seem both playful and firm.

'Do we?' The prospect gave her a deepening sense of alarm. 'I thought we discussed it all already.'

'There are a few salient details I'd like to go over,' he replied easily. 'And after tomorrow, aren't we both living there, anyway?'

'Wh—what? No,' she stammered. 'That was after we had the baby.' How had he not realised that? Of course they wouldn't live together until they needed to. *Right?* 'There's no need to live together *now*, Christos,' she told him, her tone turning almost stern.

'Well, it might help with the baby-making,' he replied dryly. 'Don't you think?'

'We're going to a *hotel*.' It was important to her that their union took place on neutral territory. She

fee table, looking utterly relaxed as well as potently virile. When she drew a breath, she inhaled the scent of his aftershave and it made something warm uncurl inside her, spread outwards. 'Christos?' she prompted.

He raised his eyebrows. 'So, no lentil salad for me?'

'I'm not even hungry any more,' she replied honestly. His arrival had completely thrown her for a loop, which he had to realise.

'That's all right,' he told her with a smile. 'I'm not either.' He patted the seat next to him. 'Why don't you come here?'

Lana was eyeing the seat next to him as if a boa constrictor were curled up on it. What was she so scared of? Well, it didn't matter, because he was determined to allay her fears, whatever they were. That was what this was about. Mostly.

He patted the cushion next to him again. 'Lana, please come sit down.'

She was still eyeing the sofa, looking uncertain, even suspicious. 'What did you mean, go into that—that meeting cold?'

'Come sit down and I'll tell you.'

'Fine.' She tossed her head, bravado back in place, and sat down next to him, her body as taut as a bow, practically quivering. It was hard not to steal a glimpse downward—that T-shirt was so worn it was nearly transparent, and although she kept folding her arms across her chest to hide it, he was pretty sure she wasn't wearing a bra. The sweatpants she wore were baggy and loose, almost falling off her slender hips. Her hair was in loose tumbled waves about her shoulders. He didn't think she'd ever looked so desirable, so *sexy*.

'Tough day at work?' Christos asked and she shrugged.

'No more than usual.'

'How are your feet?'

'What?' She looked startled. 'I saw the stilettos by the door. Killer shoes, quite literally. Do your feet hurt?'

Another shrug. 'No more than usual.'

'Come here.'

'What?'

Smiling a little, he reached for her leg. She was too surprised to resist, and he drew it up, so her foot rested in his lap.

'What…?' Her voice was unsteady, her breathing a little uneven. Already she was responding to him, and he liked it. 'What are you doing?'

'Giving you a foot massage. If you want me to?'

'Well…' She hesitated, and then shrugged her assent. 'I… I guess.'

With his thumb he started to work the muscles in the arch of her foot. After a second's surprise, a small groan of pleasure escaped her, and she let out a little laugh, clearly embarrassed at making such a sound.

'That feels really good,' she admitted, her voice still unsteady.

'Good.' Christos continued to work at her foot, watching her sideways to see how she was responding. Slowly her body began to relax. She leaned back against the sofa cushions with a sigh, and when he reached for her other foot and started on that one as well, her eyes fluttered closed.

'You're really good at this.'

He continued to work his thumbs into the sweep of her foot's arch, applying enough pressure to get at the tense muscles, to feel them relax. It was torture for him, a painful yet exquisite torture. He shifted slightly in his seat, so her foot wasn't brushing a certain part of his anatomy that was tensing even as she became more relaxed. 'Thank you.'

'Have you done it lots of times before?'

He smiled a little, even as he fought a sigh. 'As it happens, yes. But not the way you think.'

Her eyes opened and she lifted her head from the pillows to look at him. 'What do you mean?'

'My sisters used to pay me to give them foot massages. A dollar a pop. It was a nice little earner, when I was young.'

'So, this isn't your way to warm up the ladies?' she asked as she closed her eyes. 'I suppose you don't even need to. They're all willing enough.'

'Well, I certainly wouldn't take anyone to bed who was unwilling,' he replied dryly. Which was what this was about, essentially. He kept working at her feet, as her body became more pliant. He half wondered if she was falling asleep, and that was definitely *not* what he wanted.

A few minutes passed in comfortable quiet, his thumbs rotating circles on the soles of her feet. He glanced down at her, her eyes closed, her golden hair spread across the white pillow, reminding him of Sleeping Beauty. Underneath her thin T-shirt he could see the shape of her breasts, as round as apples, each one a perfect handful. He let himself look, because her eyes were closed, and the truth was he *had* to drink her in. She really had the most *beguiling* body. He ached to touch more than her foot, but that was where he kept his hands. For now.

'So, what did you mean,' she asked sleepily, her eyes still closed, 'when you said it wouldn't be good to go into our…our meeting cold?'

'Well.' He paused reflectively, sliding his hand from her foot to her ankle, curling his fingers around those slender bones, waiting for her response. Her permission. A soft sigh of assent escaped her, and he started to stroke down from her ankle, towards her foot. Wrap his fingers around her foot and then slide back up again, slowly, so slowly, towards her ankle, her skin warm and silky beneath his fingers.

This was *killing* him. He kept doing it.

'Christos?' she prompted, her eyes still closed, her body so very relaxed.

'Right. Yes.' Again, he had to shift in his seat. 'Well,' he said, continuing to stroke from foot to ankle, 'we've been married for three years, and we've barely touched each other. We've never even kissed.'

Lana tensed briefly, her foot flexing beneath his hand, and then she made herself relax. 'That was the point, though.'

'But it's not any more.'

'Tomorrow—'

'Tomorrow, yes, exactly. We go from zero to one hundred in the space of one evening? You might think I'm the king of one-night stands, but that's no way to conduct a marriage. I thought we ought to… get to know each other…a little better tonight, so tomorrow doesn't come as so much of an almighty shock.'

He glanced at her, his hand resting on her ankle, and saw her eyes wide open, bright with shock as she stared at him. 'Get to know each other?' she repeated.

'Yes.' He smiled and stroked the curve of her ankle with a single fingertip, like the touch of a butterfly. 'Get to know each other.'

She gestured to her feet in his lap. '*That's* what this is?'

'Is that a problem?'

'I thought you were giving me a foot massage!'

'Well, as you can see,' he replied equably, rubbing the arch of her foot again, 'I am.'

A shuddering breath escaped her as she slouched down against the cushions again and he continued to rub. 'What…what do you actually mean by that?' she asked. 'What…?' She licked her lips, making desire dart fiercely through him. 'What is it that you want to do?'

Everything.

His body was raging with desire now, but he kept his voice mild and soft. 'Nothing you don't want to do,' he replied. 'And anything and everything that you do.' He trailed his fingertip from the arch of her foot to her ankle, drawing circles along her skin as a shudder escaped her. 'You're in control of this, Lana, just as you like to be.'

A wobbly laugh escaped her as she slid a little further down on the sofa, so her body was basically splayed before him. 'Funny, but I don't feel in control.'

'Well, I promise you, you are.' And meanwhile he was keeping his own self-control tightly leashed—and it was getting more challenging by the minute. 'Shall I keep rubbing your feet?' he suggested, and wordlessly she nodded.

They had all night, he reminded himself, if that was what she needed. He'd come to her house this evening with no expectations but to touch her and, more importantly, have her want him to touch her. And he'd succeeded in that, but, heaven help him, he wouldn't mind moving on from her feet, lovely as they were.

He kept rubbing, then sliding his hands up to her ankles, back down again. Tormenting himself with this simple touch, never mind her.

Was she feeling it? He thought she was. Her breathing was a little uneven, her eyes still closed, a flush staining her elegant cheekbones. Every so often and she'd slide a little farther down on the sofa, her body becoming a little more open.

He decided to risk a little more, and the next time when he slid his hand from her foot to her ankle, he went a little higher, to her lower calf, her skin warm and supple beneath his questing hand. He waited again, for permission. She went still, and then her breath came out in a little shudder. Her feet relaxed in his lap, toes pushing against him in a way that *really* didn't help with his self-control. He adjusted his position once more, and then started sliding his hand from her calf to her ankle, and then back up again. Wrapping his fingers around her calf as the baggy cuff of her sweatpants slid up towards her knee, and then down again. And again. And again.

His groin throbbed and ached. Her skin was creamily golden, and his fingers slid against her like silk. A soft groan escaped her, and then a little laugh.

'I just realised I haven't even shaved,' she told him. 'I booked a wax for tomorrow morning.'

He laughed softly. 'Trust me, I don't care about that.'

She shook her head, her eyes still closed. 'You've never seen me like this.'

'I know,' he replied softly, and slid his hand up to her knee.

CHAPTER SEVEN

LANA'S BREATH HITCHED audibly as she felt Christos's hand wrap around her knee. Her whole body felt like melted butter, deliciously soft and relaxed even as an ache of longing was radiating out from her core, all the way to the tips of her toes and her fingers, gaining in strength with every passing second. She wanted him to touch her. She *needed* him to touch her. More.

His hand stayed on her knee. Every time he'd moved it, he'd paused, silently asking for her permission, and every time she'd given it, willingly, helplessly, with a little sigh or a shudder. This time was no different. He'd moved from her foot to ankle, ankle to calf and now calf to knee, but it wasn't enough. Silently she willed him to slide it higher. She didn't have the courage to say the words, but, oh, how she wanted him to do it.

Touch me. Touch me.

After several agonisingly wonderful moments, he did. Just two inches up from her knee, his hand splayed against the sensitive skin of her inner thigh, which quivered under his touch. Again, he waited. Lana's blood was pulsing now, her whole body, too, with need.

Touch me.

She scooted herself a little closer to him, her bent leg like an offering, his hand still on her lower thigh. Slowly, so slowly she knew she could make him stop at any time, he slid his hand underneath her sweatpants, along the warm expanse of her thigh, his fingers spread wide, seeking. Higher and higher, each millimetre an endless, exquisite torture, until he stopped so the tips of his fingers were almost, but not quite, brushing her hipbone.

The leg he was touching was still bent, her foot in his lap, and with her breath hitching, she let her knee fall open a little, hoping he sensed the silent invitation, feeling reckless and wanton simply for that one little act.

His hand was still high on her thigh, fingers wide. Lana felt her heart thud.

Slide it upwards, she thought. *A little more. Please. Please.*

He didn't move it. Instinctively she arched her hips just a little, lifting them up in invitation, unable to keep herself from it. She heard a shudder escape him, and she opened her eyes. He was staring straight at her, in a way that made heat and longing flood through her body. Colour slashed his cheekbones, and his breathing was uneven.

'Do you want me to touch you?' he asked in a low

voice, and she nodded. 'Tell me,' he said, his tone turning urgent. 'Tell me that you do.'

'I do,' she whispered.

'Where?'

Her heart was racing now, her mind spinning, her whole body both aching and fizzing with a longing she knew she'd never felt before.

'There...' she whispered, and slowly, his gaze still fastened on hers, he moved his hand from her thigh to the warm, pulsing centre of her, his hand slipping under her panties, his palm pressing against her gently, covering her completely, his gaze not straying from hers.

It felt like the most intimate thing Lana had ever experienced, to have his hand there. Her breath was coming in short pants, and she couldn't look away from him. He continued to press his hand against her, gently, each time sending a fiery bolt of pleasure shooting through her. She wanted more, so much more, and yet she wanted him to keep doing this for ever.

Press. Press.

Her eyes fluttered closed.

'Look at me,' Christos said in a low thrum of a voice, and she made herself open her eyes. His own eyes were glittering, his pupils dilated, his face flushed. Slowly, he slid one fingertip to flex, poised at her entrance.

Lana gulped, her body starting to tense.

'Okay?' he asked, and she wondered how he

knew. How had he understood how slowly she would need to go, how in control she would need to feel?

She nodded. 'Yes,' she whispered. 'Okay.'

Slowly, so slowly, he slid his finger inside her, the feel of it shockingly intimate. At first, she didn't feel any pleasure, just the sense of invasion, but then Christos started to stroke her, gently yet with tender persuasion, with such intimate and sure knowledge, finding that little nub of pleasure and stroking it deftly until she felt as if she were being wound tighter and tighter and then suddenly everything burst open.

Her whole body convulsed, and she felt as if she went out of her mind for a few seconds, her muscles banding around his sliding finger, her eyes rolling back as she heard herself moan in a way she never, ever had before, her hips arching against his hand, offering herself up to him as she shuddered from the force of the pleasure he'd evoked in her.

After a few seconds, the waves of pleasure receded in a tide of feeling, and she blinked up at him, her body sated yet still wanting more, shocked at how he'd touched her, how she'd responded.

She'd never, ever responded like that before. She'd never had an intimate experience of pleasure, of surrender, that hadn't involved some kind of humiliation.

'You're lousy in bed, Lana.' How many times had Anthony told her that?

The realisation of what Christos had been able to evoke and reveal in her—and so swiftly and thoroughly—was mind-blowing, and not, she realised, in a good way. She'd been so vulnerable, so exposed, helpless beneath his clever, knowing hands, and he'd *known* it. He could have done *anything* to her, and she would have agreed. Begged him, even, just as she had with Anthony. His finger was still inside her.

She twisted away from him, wincing a little as he withdrew his hand, adjusting her sweatpants as she scrambled up from the sofa, her back to him. She didn't know what the expression on her face was, but she didn't trust it.

'Lana?' he asked, and he sounded both gentle and cautious.

'You must be very proud of yourself,' she told him. She'd meant to sound wry, but her voice came out close to broken.

'Proud?' he repeated, sounding surprised and more than a little disbelieving. 'That's not actually the word I'd use right now, no.'

'You know what I mean, though.' She tucked her tumbled hair behind her ears as she forced herself to turn around and face him. 'Good for you, you've proved you're amazing in bed. Congratulations.' She folded her arms and stared him down as he gazed back, forehead furrowed.

'*That's* what you think this was about?'

'Wasn't it?'

A long, low breath escaped him as he leaned back against the sofa and raked his hands through his hair, so it flopped across his forehead. 'I suppose that's one way of looking at it,' he acknowledged slowly, 'but I meant for it to be about us becoming more comfortable with one another. So that tomorrow wasn't a complete surprise.'

'Comfortable?' she repeated scornfully. 'Comfortable would have been having a *chat*.'

'Comfortable with each other's bodies,' he clarified. There was a slight edge to his voice now, and she wondered why she was pushing him away, almost as if she wanted to make him, not *angry*, no, but not so...persuasive.

Because you're scared. Because when people get close, they hurt you. They use you.

But not Christos. She trusted him, and yet...

'Funny,' she said, 'because I wasn't touching *your* body. You were just touching mine.'

His eyes widened for a second, his irises flaring bright green, before he gestured to himself with one hand. 'Feel free to touch my body, Lana. Any time. *Please*.'

Frustration bit at her. She wasn't handling this right, lashing out in her fear and dismay at being so vulnerable, and yet she couldn't help it. 'That's not what I mean.'

'What do you mean?'

'I... I don't want to be used.'

'Used?' He stared at her in absolute incredulity, with a hint of anger. 'How was I using you, Lana? You were on board with everything I was doing. I made sure of it. I have *always* made sure of it.'

Suddenly she felt near tears. What was *wrong* with her? 'I know,' she whispered. 'I *know*.'

He stared at her for a long moment. 'What's really going on here?' he asked quietly. There was a dejectedness to his tone that tore at her.

I don't want to mess this up, she realised. *I don't want to sabotage this just because I'm scared.*

Slowly, she made herself sit back down on the sofa. She folded her hands in her lap and gazed down at them, trying to organise her jumbled, panicky thoughts. 'I'm sorry,' she said quietly. 'I'm acting like I'm unhinged. I do realise that.'

'Not unhinged,' Christos replied after a moment, his tone turning thoughtful. 'But what's really going on? Because if I were using you, Lana, trust me, I would have got a bit more satisfaction for myself.' He made his tone wry, but she had the sense that it cost him. 'Don't get me wrong,' he continued, 'I loved seeing you come apart under my touch, but, truth be told, I'm a *little* uncomfortable here.' He smiled wryly, and she flushed.

'I'm sorry.'

'Don't be.' His voice was gentle as he reached for her hand, caught it in his own. 'Tell me what's going on. Because if we want even a chance at making this work, I need to know.'

This wasn't part of their deal, Christos thought as he waited for Lana to speak, still holding her hand. He didn't *want* to know what made her tick, that was the whole point. If she'd had a bad experience, if there was some pain or trauma in her past that made her scared of sex, he didn't want to know because he already knew he wouldn't be able to deal with it.

So why was he asking? Why, right now, did he want her to tell him?

'Lana?'

'I've…had a few bad relationships,' she confessed. 'One in particular. I guess it's…affected my perception.'

'Of sex?'

'Yes. Of sex. Of intimacy. Of…everything.'

It wasn't actually, he realised, something he hadn't known, or at least suspected, even if she'd never told him the particulars. Her wary, ice-cold attitude to physical intimacy had been something of a giveaway, after all. 'Tell me about it?' he invited, even as he wondered why he was asking. He didn't want to ask. He didn't want to know. And yet here he was.

She stared at him for a moment, golden brows drawn together, clearly conflicted. 'I didn't think this was part of our deal.'

He raised his eyebrows. 'Knowing our personal histories?'

'Getting close.'

'This isn't falling in love, Lana, this is just being forewarned. I don't want to make any more mistakes, since it seems I did make one tonight.'

To his deep dismay, her eyes filled with tears, one almost slipping down her cheek before she brushed at it with her hand. He was so not good with tears. 'You didn't make any mistakes, Christos.'

'I feel like I did.'

'Well, trust me, you didn't. No one has made me feel the way you did.' She bit her lip, a smile lurking in her eyes now along with the tears. 'I hope that doesn't freak you out.'

'It doesn't.' Truth be told, it made him feel like a million bucks. 'But what happened to you?'

A sigh escaped her, long and shuddery. 'All right, I'll tell you. It's only fair. But I think I need a glass of wine first.'

'All right.'

She slipped from the sofa and disappeared into the kitchen, while Christos leaned back against the sofa and closed his eyes. This had all got a bit intense. He'd come here with one agenda, and one agenda only—to make Lana respond to him physically. To open her up like a flower and let her enjoy the unfurling. But he hadn't intended for it to become emotional at *all*, and yet here they were.

He couldn't back away now. Not the way he had with his mother, his sisters—shutting down when they needed him most, walking away when they'd asked, even begged, him not to. He'd thought he'd be different with Lana, because his emotions weren't engaged.

And they weren't, he reminded himself, so he could handle this conversation. He could help her, without feeling anything himself. This was all about the physical, anyway. Making sure Lana enjoyed sex.

As long as they kept it that way, it would be fine. He would be.

She came back into the room, a wine bottle in

one hand, a pair of glasses in the other. 'I brought two,' she said, brandishing the glasses, 'in case you wanted some?'

He shrugged, smiled. 'Sure.'

She must have sensed something a little off about his tone, because she cocked her head, her blue, blue gaze sweeping slowly over him. 'Are you all right?'

'Yes, of course.' He didn't sound all right. He was starting to get freaked out, although not for the reason Lana thought. He loved knowing he'd been able to make her respond to his touch, but he didn't want her to respond to him like *this*. Telling him her secrets. Sharing her pain. Yet how the hell could he explain that?

I'm fine, but don't talk about your trauma, because you know what? I can't handle it.

'I'm fine,' he said, but Lana did not look convinced. She opened the bottle of wine and poured them both glasses, handing him his before curling up on one end of the sofa with hers.

'Do you want me to tell you about this?' she asked, and he raised his wine glass to his lips.

'Only if you want to.'

She pursed her lips, looking at him hard, and Christos had the sense she knew exactly what was happening, how he was backing away again, unable to keep himself from it, even though he wished he could. 'All right,' she replied finally. 'I'll give you the basics.'

'Okay.' He already knew he wouldn't ask for more.

She took a sip of wine, swallowing it slowly as

she composed her thoughts. Christos waited, bracing himself, knowing he had to get his reaction right, and already fearing he wouldn't be able to.

'There was a guy,' she said at last, her gaze on her glass. 'A man. I was young, very young. Twenty-one, just out of university, starting my first internship.' She paused, her lips pursed, her forehead furrowed in thought. For a second Christos let himself simply enjoy how lovely she looked—her hair tumbled about her shoulders in artless waves, not the smooth, gleaming sheet it usually was. Her face devoid of make-up, her T-shirt sliding off one slender, golden shoulder. She was such a beautiful woman, and no more so when she wasn't even thinking about it, using it to her advantage with her power suits, stiletto heels.

'I presume you're going to give me a few more details than that,' he remarked when she hadn't spoken for some time.

'Yes, a few.' She nodded, seeming brisk now, professional, her voice devoid of any of the emotion he'd been fearing.

So why was he disappointed?

His own contrary nature annoyed him, and he pushed the thought away.

'He was my first—lover, I suppose, although I don't even like using that word with him, but I did love him. I was besotted with him, actually.'

She grimaced, and Christos found he didn't like hearing about that. *Besotted?* Really?

'He was ten years older than me, an advertising

executive I'd met through work. He was very charming—charismatic, snappy dresser, full of energy. I'm sure you know the type, especially in advertising.' She glanced up at him, smiling wryly, and Christos gave a terse nod.

Yes, he knew the type. Fake, smarmy bastards with their shiny Rolexes and loud laughs.

'Anyway.' A sigh escaped her, her shoulders slumping a little. 'I was…bewitched. That's what it felt like, that's what it was. If he'd told me to jump, I would have asked how high, and then I would have tried to jump higher.'

'You were young,' he said, when it seemed as if a reply was needed. He felt like punching this guy, whoever he was, right in the face.

'Well, that's the background,' Lana told him.

She was looking at him now, her eyes hard, her face like a mask. *No emotion here.*

'And the reality is that sex, intimacy, was something of a weapon to him, one he used to his advantage every time. And the—the bedroom became a place to be humiliated, even to be hurt. And I allowed that to happen.' Her voice, although as hard as his eyes, wavered a little at the last, and she took a quick sip of wine.

Christos stared at her, realisation thudding sickly inside him. He didn't want to punch this smarmy bastard now, he thought. He wanted to kill him.

'Lana…' He didn't actually know what to say. What to do. He wanted to offer her comfort, understanding, take her in his arms and gently kiss the tears he could see gathering in her eyes even as she determinedly blinked them back. He *wanted* to, but he didn't. Couldn't. It was as if he were frozen in place, his mind shutting down, his heart too.

I can't handle this.

He simply stared at her, and he saw understanding gleam in her eyes briefly, like a light being switched on and then just as quickly off. She nodded slowly.

'So now you know,' she said, and it felt like the end of the conversation.

It was the end, because she clambered off the sofa, taking her glass into the kitchen, while he simply sat there, his mind spinning, his heart heavy as a stone. When she came back into the room, she looked composed, calm.

'If you want to stay the night,' she said, 'you can use the guest room downstairs.'

Oof. As if that weren't a brush-off, after what they'd just shared. Except, he realised, they hadn't actually shared anything. He'd made sure of it.

'All right,' he replied, equably enough, because the last thing he was going to do was insist on anything. Still, he felt duty-bound to ask, 'Tomorrow still good?'

She stared at him for a beat, her expression stony, the smile she gave brittle. 'Oh, yes,' she said. 'Tomorrow's still good.'

CHAPTER EIGHT

LANA SLID ONTO the stool at the hotel's swanky cocktail bar, wriggling a little in the LBD she'd chosen to wear—an elegant sheath of rippling black silk, sleeves, with a square neckline, hitting just above her knee. She'd sometimes worn it to work paired with a blazer, but it could also function as an evening dress, when she was out and about for business.

Which was what tonight was, after all.

'Can I get you something, ma'am?' the bartender asked, and Lana gave him a quick smile.

'Snake Bite, please.'

As ever, a gleam of admiration entered the guy's eyes. Women who drank whisky were always held in high esteem, Lana had noticed, but that wasn't why she ordered the drink. She just liked whisky. 'Coming right up,' he said, and she swivelled on her stool to survey the room.

Christos was due to meet her here in ten minutes. She'd come early, needing the time to compose herself, stake out her ground. She'd already been upstairs to check on the hotel suite, make sure the staff hadn't done anything romantic to it. No champagne chilling in a bucket, no rose petal scattered across satin sheets, thank you very much. Fortunately, the staff had followed her requests and the hotel room looked exactly as she wanted it to look—elegant but functional.

They were *not*, she'd already decided, going to have a repeat of last night. Oh, she wasn't going to go out of her way to avoid any pleasure, even if the idea of exposing herself again, feeling so vulnerable, so helpless under his hands, made her feel more than a little nervous. But the emotional side of things, when she'd talked about Anthony, when she'd told Christos how she'd been hurt—and then had seen the frozen look on his face? Nope. That was definitely not happening again.

Tonight it was all business, and it would be very pleasurable business indeed—but it was still business.

'Here's your drink, ma'am.' The bartender slid the tumbler across the bar, and Lana took it with murmured thanks before tossing it back in one burning swallow. The man whistled softly under his breath. 'You're some sexy lady there.'

She gave him a quick, quelling look. The last thing she needed right now was that sort of comment. She'd been dealing with them all her life, since she'd hit puberty at all of eleven years old, and she'd learned that ignoring such remarks, while not always the most satisfying of choices, usually had the best chance of success.

Fortunately, she'd just seen Christos stride through the hotel's lobby, and so she tossed a twenty onto the bar and walked away. His eyes gleamed as he caught sight of her coming towards him, but she sensed in him a hidden reserve, and she knew it was because of what she'd told him last night. Why on earth had she done that? Well, she certainly wouldn't do it again tonight. Or ever.

'Hello there, husband.' Her smile was playful, her voice light, as she cocked her head. She knew how she wanted to play this now. How it needed to be. 'I've made a dinner reservation in the hotel's restaurant. Apparently, they do an excellent filet mignon.'

'Do they?' He arched an eyebrow, looking far too gorgeous in his navy-blue suit, a paler blue shirt and a silvery-grey tie. His hair was rumpled, his jaw freshly shaven even though it was six o'clock in the evening, and he smelled fantastic. 'Why don't we eat after?'

'What?' The word slipped out, a single syllable of shock and dismay, before she could stop it.

He shrugged, his eyes dancing, his smile slow and sure as his sleepy gaze lingered on hers. 'I'm not that hungry.'

For food.

He didn't say it, but she felt as if he had. A shiver ran along her skin, and her stomach clenched with both nerves and anticipation. This was not how she'd expected the evening to go. They were supposed to wine and dine each other, talk shop, laugh and chat, and by the time they went upstairs she would feel firmly in control of who she was—and who she wasn't. And she would stay that way even as Christos peeled the clothes from her body, even as he played her body like an instrument, coaxing a tune of pleasure from every inch of her. It would be *business*.

But clearly that was not how this was going to go, because Christos was already turning towards the bank of elevators.

'Wait,' she said, and he turned back, waiting.

'Why the rush?' she asked, forcing her voice to sound light. 'We need to eat.'

'Why not just get on with it?' he challenged with a small shrug. 'Because if we don't, you'll be winding yourself up all evening, getting less and less relaxed, not more so, which I know is what you think will happen, but trust me, it won't. You'll agonise about everything and by the time we're eating dessert, you'll be ready to snap.' His mouth curved into a slow smile. 'Not exactly the best way to start a seduction.'

It was true, Lana knew. She *would* get tense, even tenser than she already was. He knew her so well, better than she knew herself. He started walking towards the elevators, his stride long and sure.

'You don't even know what room it is,' she called after him, 'or what floor.'

He slid a card out of his jacket pocket and held it up. 'I have a key.'

'*What?* How do you have a key?'

'I'm your husband. I asked for one at the desk, and they gave it to me.' He made it sound simple, but Lana suspected he'd had to do some smooth talking to get a key to the room that was reserved in her name only.

Whenever she thought she was in control, Lana realised, whenever she let herself believe that for so much as a second, Christos demonstrated otherwise.

'Why do you need a key?' she half grumbled as she followed him towards the elevators.

He glanced at her, his eyebrows raised. 'Why don't you want me to have one?'

'It's not that.' It was a petty argument, and one she didn't actually care about, except…she was trying to control things. And he wasn't letting her. Why?

'Well?' he asked, eyebrows still raised, as they stood in front of the elevators. 'Are we going to go or not?'

Now, *right* now, upstairs, and then… She tilted her chin, let her gaze flash challenge. 'Why not?'

The answering smile he gave her made her stomach swoop and her toes curl. Why not, indeed.

The ride upwards was utterly silent, an expectation building that felt like a pressure in her chest, a loosening between her thighs. Her heart was starting to race with treacherous excitement, her palms turning damp with nerves.

This was happening. This was actually happening.

Christos stepped aside so she could leave the elevator first, and then he strode down the corridor, to the suite at the end. He didn't just have the key; he knew where the room was. Had he been in there before she had? Or after? She hadn't actually seen him enter the hotel, Lana realised, just in the lobby. What had he done?

'Have you already been in the room?' she asked.

'Maybe,' he replied, and swiped the card, opening the door so she stepped in first. She glanced around the suite, and saw, at least, there were no romantic rose petals on the bed. There *was* a bottle of champagne chilling, so, clearly, he had been here. She didn't know how she felt about that, but before she could so much as think about it, he'd put his hands on her shoulders and was turning her around, slowly but purposefully, so she was facing him, a look of intent darkening his hazel gaze.

Her breath caught in her chest. In the same slow, deliberate way, he backed her up against the wall. She hit it with a gentle thud, surprise slamming through her with far more force. This was not what she'd expected, either.

Christos slid his hands from her bare shoulders to frame her face, fingers splayed across her jawbone, in a caress that felt achingly tender.

'I'm going to kiss you,' he said. 'Okay?'

Wordlessly she nodded. His mouth settled on hers, their first kiss ever, soft as velvet, tender at first but then with demand, with knowledge, with urgency. His tongue traced her lips as he deepened the kiss and she felt as if a hand had plunged right into her chest, shaken everything up, left her both gasping for air and wanting more.

He pressed against her, so her back was flat against the wall, the hard length of his arousal fitting into the juncture of her thighs, thrilling her, shocking her, because already, one kiss in, and he very clearly wanted her. A lot.

And she didn't know what to do with that information.

She put her hands on his shoulders, more to brace herself than anything else, but then he laid his hands on top of hers and drew them up, so they were straight above her head, against the wall. She stared at him with shocked eyes as he pressed the entire length of his body, from fingertip to toe, against her, every inch of her covered by every inch of him.

It felt like a complete physical and emotional overload—once she might have felt trapped by the hard body against hers, but right then she simply felt covered, and not just covered, but shielded. Protected, and even known. And that sensation shook her to her very core. She closed her eyes as he rocked his hips against hers, in the same sort of gentle movement that he'd pressed his hand against her last night, and in the same way she felt herself go boneless with wanting, her breath ragged with need.

Amazingly, his breath was even more ragged than hers. That, she realised, she hadn't expected. At all.

Christos drew his hands down from hers, sliding them all along her body before anchoring them on her hips. Touching her was exquisite agony, and he wanted her to know it. He wanted her to know how much she affected him.

He'd spent several hours last night in her guest

room, an ache in his groin as well as his heart as he'd thought about all she'd said—and revealed. She thought she needed to be in control in the bedroom, because she hadn't been before, with that utter jerk of a guy who Christos could hardly bear to think of. Being in control made Lana feel safe, and he understood that. And yet, Christos had realised while lying alone in bed, he'd given her all the control last night. He'd made sure she was calling the shots, giving her consent at absolutely every juncture, and she'd still felt...*used.* It was a word that did not sit well with him. At all.

That was when he'd realised that maybe Lana didn't want so much to feel in control as to see *him* losing it. Not being calculating and cold the way that jerk of a boyfriend had been, but needing and desiring her completely. She needed to see and believe that he wanted her so much it drove him crazy, because it did. Last night he'd kept his own self-control tightly leashed. He'd never shown her how much he desired her, had been entirely focused on her pleasure, thinking, genuinely believing it was the way to make this work between them.

But maybe it wasn't. And tonight, he was trying something else. With his hands on her hips, he slowly drew her dress up to her waist, and a gasp escaped her. She was wearing sheer black stockings and black lace garters, sexy as hell. Christos pushed against her a little more, like a question, and another gasp escaped her, her head falling back against the wall. He kissed her throat, reaching around the back of her dress to drag the zip down. The dress slithered from her shoulders and then with one restless shrug, it pooled at her feet.

He eased back to look at her—black lace bra and pants, those sheer stockings, stilettos, *garters*. 'You're killing me,' he told her on a shaky breath, and she let out an unsteady laugh.

'I was actually going to change. I have a very respectable negligee—'

'Later.' He was kissing her again, from her mouth to her throat to the delightful vee between her breasts, her skin silken against his lips, his hands still on her hips, anchoring him against her. Her hands roamed across his back, and then slid under his shirt, against his heated skin. That touch alone nearly undid him. A groan escaped him, and her eyes widened as she looked at him, a silent question.

'I want you so much,' he told her. 'I know this is just the beginning, but I'm not sure how much longer I'm going to hold out, to be honest.'

It was a somewhat humbling admission, but he thought it was one she needed to hear, and in any case it was true. He felt just about ready to explode. 'Really?' she exclaimed dazedly, her face flushed, pupils dilated, and he let out a shaky laugh as he slid his hand along the bare, silky skin between her panties and stocking, pulling her leg around his hip and thrusting against her with delicious intent.

'Really.'

Her breath was coming in pants now as she rocked

back against him. 'Well, I guess…' she whispered as she continued to move. 'I guess that would be okay.'

'Good.' If he'd wanted to romance her a little more, well, too bad. This was what he needed—to be inside her, hard and hot and fast. He hoped it was what she needed, too.

He guided her hand to his belt. 'Undo it for me,' he managed in a rasp. 'Please.'

Her fingers trembling a little, she fumbled with the buckle, and then, with a snick of leather, he was free. She pushed down his trousers, her fingers barely skimming the length of him, but it was enough to almost make him lose control.

Not yet.

Not quite yet. He pushed aside her panties, positioned himself, pulsing and so very ready, at her core. She arched up and he waited for one agonising second.

'Are you ready?'

'Yes.'

That was all he needed. He drove into her in one smooth stroke, a gasp escaping him as he felt her close around him and they began to move in sync, one stroke after another, each one driving him higher, wilder. He wanted to wait, he *had* to wait until he felt her climax, he knew that much, but, heaven help him, it felt near impossible.

He was close, *so* close, his whole body shuddering, his breath coming in gasps as she folded herself around him, her lips pressed against his throat, her leg around his hip, her hands roaming almost frantically along his back.

And then Lana let out a cry and her body shuddered around his and Christos let himself go. The release was immense, overwhelming his whole body, flooding his senses.

'Lana,' he heard himself saying, over and over. 'Lana. *Lana.*'

Eventually, after what surely was only a few seconds but felt like minutes or even hours, the waves of pleasure receded, leaving them both sticky and sated, their clothing and hair rumpled, their breathing still uneven.

With a self-conscious smile, Lana began to untangle herself from him, unwinding her leg from around his hip, and then, to his surprise, sliding slowly to the floor.

She shook her head, a trembling laugh escaping her as she slid right down to the ground, still in just her rucked-up underwear, drawing her knees up to her chest, letting her head fall onto them. Christos watched her uneasily, his heart still thudding from the aftershocks of the most incredible orgasm he'd ever had. What if he hadn't handled this right? Had he scared her? Hurt her? He'd never forgive himself, he knew that much.

'Lana…' he began, and then realised he didn't know what to say.

Her head was still resting on her knees. 'I…' she began, and then looked up, her face flushed as she smiled wryly. *'Wow.'*

Christos felt a huge grin spreading over his face. *Success.*

'Yeah,' he agreed as he held out a hand to her and helped her up from the floor. 'Wow.'

'I've never…' she began, scrambling to her feet. She reached for her dress, but only to toss it on a chair. He could get used to seeing her in just her bra and pants, and definitely those garters. 'I have *never* felt like that before,' she told him frankly, and warmth bloomed in his chest, along with the pride she'd accused him of last night. But he knew it wasn't the macho pride of another notch on the bedpost; no, it was something deeper and more elemental than that. He'd *reached* her. He'd touched her, in a way nobody else had been able to, and yes, for that, he felt proud. Proud and touched himself.

And, he realised, a little freaked out, but he wasn't going to dwell on that particular emotion now. He just wanted to enjoy this moment, in all of its resounding glory.

'Well,' he told her as he pulled up his trousers with a smile, 'I actually haven't, either.'

'Oh, come on, you have.' She spoke carelessly, but with a sting in the words that he felt.

Not this again.

She stood in front of him, her lithe, golden body resplendent in all that black lace, hands on her hips, her hair tumbled about her shoulders. 'You probably do twice a week, at least.'

'Seriously, Lana?' He didn't want to argue, and certainly not now, but twice a *week*?

'I'm not accusing you of anything,' she replied, even though it sort of felt as if she was. 'Just…let's be realistic. You're good at sex. I mean, own it, Christos. You know your way around a woman.' She smiled and shrugged, and it felt, surprisingly, like a rather brutal brush-off.

This, he realised, was another way she distanced herself, and if he was smart, he would take it, so they could both stick to the terms of their deal. No emotional engagement, but yes, lots of great sex, because, hell, maybe he was good at it. So was she, even if she didn't know it.

This was when he should say, *Why, thank you very much, and let me prove it to you again.*

But the words, so laughing and light, didn't come.

'Actually,' he told her as he tucked his shirt in, his tone more matter-of-fact than wry, 'I may be good at sex, but before tonight I hadn't had it in three years.'

CHAPTER NINE

LANA STARTED TO SMILE, only to see that Christos was utterly serious. She felt the smile slide off her face like a pancake off a plate as she stared at him, incredulous, uncertain, appalled, *hopeful*. The jumble of her emotions felt like too much to process.

'What?' she said finally. 'You're…' She meant to say joking, but at the sight of the almost sombre look on his face, she found she couldn't.

'I'm serious,' he replied in the affable tone he so often used, but she sensed something underneath—an uncertainty, perhaps, or a defensiveness. 'Although admittedly, it wasn't for lack of trying, at least at first.'

She frowned, unsure how she felt about that. 'What is that supposed to mean, exactly?'

He shrugged as he walked into the bedroom, towards the champagne. Lana watched him peel the foil from the cork and realised she was still only in her underwear, and right then it felt a little…exposing. She grabbed the thick, velvety-soft robe off the back of the bathroom door and shrugged into it, the heavy material enveloping her like one of the fur coats from the kids in Narnia.

'Christos?' she prompted when it didn't seem as if he was going to say anything more.

'When we first made our deal,' he explained carefully, his gaze on the bottle of champagne he was opening, 'I thought I'd do exactly what you'd suggested, and have…liaisons. Very discreet, very brief ones. It seemed reasonable, considering our arrangement as well as your own suggestion, and I decided it didn't go against my personal ethics.'

No surprises there, then. Lana folded her arms and waited for more. Christos popped the cork on the champagne and then neatly poured two flutes right to the top, managing to make sure that the fizz didn't overflow.

'Very nicely done,' she murmured, and he gave her a quick, rakish smile before handing her a glass. 'To us,' he said, and Lana clinked glasses.

'To us,' she agreed, although she wondered what aspect of *us* he was referring to. The deal they'd made three years, or three days ago? The incredible sex they'd just had, which she was still reeling from? 'So, you tried to have a…liaison,' she stated after she'd taken a sip of the crisp bubbles, realising she didn't actually like to imagine it in any detail. 'What happened?'

Christos grimaced wryly. 'Well, I won't embarrass myself by going into the specifics, but let's just say it didn't go according to plan.'

'What does that mean?'

His grimaced deepened, although she could tell he was trying to find the humour in it. 'Let's just say I disappointed the lady in question.'

Lana was surprised to find a bubble of laughter rising up in her throat. 'Are you implying what I… think you're implying?'

Christos shrugged, his eyes sparkling over the rim of his glass as he took a sip of his champagne. 'Fortunately, this lady did not take it as a personal insult.'

'I can't believe—'

'I couldn't, either. And I don't intend to find myself in that situation ever again.' His eyes glinted into hers. 'And considering what happened just now, I don't think I will.'

Lana's stomach fizzed as much as the champagne she was drinking. No, she didn't think he would, either. Having Christos want her so much, so obviously, had been the most intoxicating aphrodisiac she'd ever experienced. She'd felt powerful in a way she never had before, powerful and desired. Two things she'd never felt with another man, and especially not Anthony. But she didn't want to think about Anthony now.

'You must have tried again,' she remarked after a moment, her lips pursed. She realised she did not like the thought of it. At all.

Christos shook his head. 'No, trust me, once was enough for that kind of experience.' He gave a not-so-mock shudder. 'In any case, after that… I realised I took my marriage vows more seriously than I'd thought.'

Lana took another sip of champagne, mainly to hide the expression on her face—not that she even knew what it was. She felt extraordinarily touched by his admission, as well as pleased, and also disconcerted. Christos was meant to be the master of no-strings sex and yet he'd abstained for three years because of the vows they'd made, back when they'd barely known each other? There seemed to be a fair amount of emotion in *that*.

'I don't know what to say,' she said at last. 'I never thought… I never expected…'

'I know.' He put his glass down. 'And to be clear, I don't hold you to the same standard, for those three years. Although going into the future is another matter entirely.'

Since he'd been so honest, she felt she had to be, too, and in truth, to her own surprise, she realised she wanted to be. How novel. How *odd*. 'I'm afraid I'm the winner if you want to play that game, Christos,' she told him with a shaky laugh. 'Because I beat you by a country mile.'

He stilled, his hazel gaze searching hers. 'Oh?'

Lana nodded. 'By quite a few years. Nine, in fact, give or take a few months.' She swallowed hard, toying with the sash of her robe. 'Although I thought you might have guessed that, based on some of my reactions.'

'Well, I suppose I wondered.' He looked down for a moment, his expression thoughtful and maybe even a little sad, and then he glanced up and a smile spread across his face, humour lighting his eyes, giving them a golden sheen. 'What a pair we are, eh? Clearly, we have a lot of lost time to make up for.'

Lana found herself smiling back, suddenly almost dizzy with something that felt like more than relief, closer to joy. 'Clearly we do.'

He closed the space between them in two prowling strides, tugging gently at the sash of her robe, until it came undone, and the robe fell away. His hands slid around her waist, spanning its width and settling there as Lana swayed towards him. Her body was still weak and relaxed from their last bout of lovemaking, but amazingly she felt ready again, and, it seemed, so did he.

'Are you going to take off your clothes this time?' she asked wryly, and his eyebrows lifted.

'Only if you'll do it for me.'

A thrill of wonder—and a little fear—rippled through her. 'I guess I can manage that.' She started to unbutton his shirt, her fingers trembling a little because, as wonderful as this was, she couldn't deny that it felt emotional. Physical intimacy *was* emotional, she realised with a jolt. How could it not be? She'd known that all along, but she'd tried to deny it—to herself and to Christos. Yet standing here in front of him, she knew she couldn't any longer. She slid her hands along the taut and sculpted muscles of his chest as she parted the folds of his shirt and he shrugged out of it, his eyes now dark with desire, his breath turned uneven once more.

Lana ran a single fingertip along his pectoral muscle and a shudder escaped him. 'You drive me crazy, you know,' he murmured in a husky voice, and she could feel how much he meant it.

'You drive me crazy, too,' she whispered, trailing her fingertip lower, past the ridges of his ribs, to the light sprinkling of hair veeing down below his waistband. Christos sucked in a breath as he wrapped his hand around her own, stilling it.

'I mean it,' he told her in a low voice. 'You really do drive me crazy.' He drew her hand upwards before he cupped her breasts with his hands, flicking his thumbs over her nipples. A shuddery gasp escaped her. 'And I'm glad I drive you crazy, too.'

It felt like a safe sentiment to say, for them both to feel, but Lana knew it wasn't. There was already too much invested in this aspect of their relationship, where they exposed and revealed, not just their bodies, but their very selves. It was too late to remedy that, she knew, and in truth she didn't even want to. Being touched by Christos felt far, far too good. She didn't think she wanted to go without the wonder of it again.

But she *could* keep the emotional side of things confined simply to sex, she decided. They wouldn't talk about their pasts again, they wouldn't share their fears or hurts, their dreams or desires, and they certainly wouldn't ever need or depend on each other in any tangible way.

She'd be able to keep *that* essential part of herself safe still, at least, in a way she hadn't been able to before. Just thinking of Anthony, the sneer that would twist his face when she begged him to listen, to love her… She would never let herself feel so humiliated and exposed again. Ever. No matter what.

'Lana.' Christos framed her face with his hands. 'What are you thinking right now?'

'What?' She glanced up at him, startled, a tremble going through her as he ran his thumb over the fullness of her lower lip.

'You suddenly got a very ferocious look on your face.'

His voice and expression were both so achingly tender that, despite the resolution she'd just made, she found herself blurting, 'I was just thinking how different this is from what I've known before, and how—how it is hard to accept that it truly is different.'

Christos's eyes darkened as he cradled her face so tenderly. 'I won't hurt you,' he said, a promise, a vow, and one she knew he believed he could make.

Lana nodded shakily. 'I know,' she said, compelled to even more honesty. 'Because I won't let you.'

Christos stared at her hard for a long moment, and then he kissed her long and deep, and Lana surrendered herself to it, because that part, at least, was easy.

Because I won't let you.

The words reverberated through Christos as he lost himself in their kiss. What the hell was that supposed to mean? He suspected she'd meant it as reassurance, if not for him then at least for herself, but he hadn't *felt* it that way. It had stung, because if anyone was going to make boundaries, it would be him. Right?

As they fell back on the bed, he told himself to stop thinking about it. He unhooked Lana's bra, drawing it away from her body so her lovely breasts were on full and wondrous display, ready for his touch. There were so many other wonderful things to think about now, after all.

An hour later, they were both sleepily sated, limbs tangled among the sheets, Lana's head resting on Christos's shoulder, her cheek against his chest, which was, he realised, exactly where he wanted her to be. He toyed with the long golden strands of her hair as they both let their breathing settle.

If he'd thought their first encounter had been explosive, their second had been even more so, but in a long and lingering way that had been just as, if not more, satisfying—and emotional.

Yes, emotional. He had to use that word, as wary as he was of it, because he could not deny that what he felt with Lana was different from what he'd felt with any other woman. Every time they came together, he felt as if he were offering a little bit of his soul. He didn't even mean to, but it happened anyway, and he didn't know whether she would accept it or not. Did she even know?

I won't let you.

Lana was clearly going to keep her heart and soul tightly locked away, Christos realised, even as she gave him everything else. And meanwhile he was starting to have the awful, sneaking suspicion that he might not be able to keep from serving his own up on a plate. It was a conundrum, but one that, oddly, wasn't bothering him too much in this moment. He simply felt too happy.

'Do you think we made a baby?' he asked her, and she let out a sleepy laugh.

'*That* would have been quick.'

'But possible.'

'Yes.' She sounded happy too, and he liked that. He liked that a lot.

'Imagine—there might already be a tiny, tiny baby nestled in there.' He slid his hand down to her flat stomach, spreading his fingers wide, feeling a ripple of desire go through him even though he was absolutely spent.

'I don't think it happens that quickly.'

'How long does it take a sperm and egg to do their thing?'

She laughed, a pure, clear sound. 'I don't actually know.'

'Me neither.'

'I could look it up on my phone,' she suggested, and, twisting away from him so he felt the loss, she walked naked to the purse she'd dropped by the door when they'd first arrived and took out her phone. Christos was aching for her to get back into bed with him, but he simply stretched out and acted nonchalant as she walked slowly back towards him, squinting at the screen of her phone.

'It takes up to forty-five minutes for the sperm to reach the egg,' she told him as she scrambled back into bed, and it felt both easy and right to stretch his arm out and draw her back to his chest, her head nestled into his shoulder. She fitted there so very nicely. 'And "up to twenty-four hours for the act of fertilisation to complete",' she read off her phone. 'So not a baby quite yet.'

'Still.'

'"The genetic make-up of the baby is complete at the moment of fertilisation,"' she read, before tossing her phone aside. 'Isn't that *crazy*? As soon as tomorrow there *could* be a tiny, tiny baby, with all its genes and everything, and all it needs to do is grow.'

'A little bit of me, a little bit of you,' Christos said, and she laughed softly, her breath fanning his chest.

'Well, fifty per cent of me, fifty per cent of you.'

'Pedant,' he teased, and she tilted her face up to him, which simply meant he had to kiss her. He'd meant to make it something between a brush and a peck, but it ended up being long and lingering instead, and his hand tightened on her shoulder as hers drifted temptingly lower.

'Lana,' he growled, and she looked at him innocently.

'What?'

'You know what,' he said as her hand went even lower and even though he'd thought he didn't have it in him for another round, he now found that he did.

'Just in case the first two times didn't take,' Lana whispered, and then her lips followed the path of her hands, and Christos found himself closing his eyes as he surrendered to the bliss.

They finished the champagne, ate lobster salad and crusty rolls and sweet, succulent strawberries dipped in chocolate, while sitting naked among the pillows and sheets, careless of crumbs. Christos couldn't remember the last time he'd felt so relaxed, so at ease—with himself, with the woman beside him, with the whole world.

This marriage thing, he decided, had been a *very* good idea. Lana seemed to think so too, even if she hadn't said as much. He'd never seen her so relaxed, either—her hair loose and wavy about her shoulders, her limbs splayed carelessly as she popped a strawberry into her mouth, juice dripping down her chin.

He liked her like this, he realised. Seeing her now, naked in bed, he realised just how tightly held and tense she was, in her normal self. From her stilettos to the gleaming sheet of her hair—it had all been armour, a way for her to face the world down, to conquer it.

But if it was armour, Christos thought with a sudden lurch of understanding, then there was something that needed protecting underneath, and he'd gone into this marriage not wanting there to be. Lana had already showed him some of her vulnerabilities—reluctantly, yes, but they were clearly there. He couldn't pretend, even to himself, that she was nothing more than the image she presented to the world—glossy, self-assured and diamond-hard.

'I think I could sleep for about twelve hours,' Lana said, stretching languorously, making Christos's libido give yet another pulse as she arched her back, lamplight dancing over her golden skin. 'It's a good thing my first meeting isn't till twelve tomorrow.' She gave him a cat-like smile before she rose from the bed and began clearing the dishes away.

After a second's pause, Christos started to help, even though his mind was still spinning. The sleepy, contented satiation he'd been experiencing all evening was stealing away, leaving cold hard truth in its wake.

Their marriage might be a good idea—but it was already also very complicated. And if he wanted to keep his head—and heart—intact, then he needed to think clearly about how he handled himself in the future. Lana seemed to have got the memo; hell, she'd written it. So he definitely needed to get on board.

He was still thinking that way as they got ready for bed a little while later; Lana had changed into the coffee-coloured silk nightgown she'd mentioned earlier, and that Christos already wanted to slide off her; he liked her naked. But she had, it seemed, reverted to her usual self, a stickler for protocol, and their honeymoon, brief as it was, seemed to be over.

'Goodnight,' she said, and kissed his cheek. They might as well have been married for fifty years.

Christos let out a growl, a purely instinctive sound, and then wrapped his hand around the back of her head so he could kiss her goodnight the way he wanted to—long and slow and deep.

'Goodnight,' he said, and she looked shaken for a second, before she smiled and turned out the light.

Christos lay on his back, one hand braced behind his head. As fatigued as he was from all their enjoyable exertions, sleep felt as if it would be a very long time coming. His feelings—yes, feelings—were a jumbled mess, and he wanted to sort them out.

Ever since he'd disappointed not just his mother, but all three of his sisters, he'd avoided any emotion, knowing he couldn't deal with it because he'd just let people down as he had before, in the worst possible way.

He didn't think he'd ever forget the agonised look on his dying mother's face. *'Please, Christos. Let me see you. Let me hug you and say goodbye to you, just one last time.'*

He'd walked away without a word. What must she have thought of him? Felt in that agonising moment? He'd never seen her again; she'd died several hours later. There were a lot of things he hadn't had a chance to say.

I'm sorry. I miss you. I love you.

And that knowledge was like a wound inside him, a festering cancer that would never, ever heal. The safest way he'd discovered of dealing with it was never giving himself an opportunity to need to say those kinds of words again. Never get close enough to someone that they'd be expected to be said. And never letting anyone down when he couldn't say them.

He twisted to look at Lana, who had already fallen

asleep, her hair spread out on the pillow, her breathing deep and even. She looked like an elegant angel.

He didn't want to let her down, he thought heavily, most of all, but it might be that he wouldn't be able to keep himself from it…just like before.

CHAPTER TEN

'So, you need to be someone different.'

Her hands folded on the desk in front of her, Lana gazed at the geeky young tech wizard who was in her office on Albert's recommendation. Thirtysomething, awkward and shy, pushing his glasses up with his forefinger, with a rather endearing stammer and a nervous blink. He'd developed an app that was poised to become huge, and he needed the image to go with it.

'Yeah, that's the plan.' The man, Jack Philips, gave her a quick, uncertain smile. 'Albert said you specialise in helping people make their mark.'

'Well, that's pretty much the point of PR,' she replied with a smile. 'Your company is new, but it's already generating some serious buzz. We can work with that, especially with a digital campaign. A personal element also works—maybe a spotlight feature in one of the newspaper's cultural supplements to highlight who you are?'

'Yeah, that might not work out so well,' Jack said with a grimace. 'My life is pretty boring.'

'Well, we can make it more interesting.' That was what she did—help people to shape their pasts, their whole selves, to be what the world wanted. It was what she'd done for herself, aged twenty-two, after she'd left Anthony and the firm where she'd interned, determined to be different, better, stronger. She knew she could do it for this guy.

He frowned, not understanding. 'How would we make it more interesting?'

'It's all in the information you reveal, the particular slant you find,' she explained.

'I grew up in New Jersey, the third son of a housewife and an insurance salesman,' he said, raising his eyebrows. 'How can you make that more interesting?'

'I can make anything more interesting,' Lana promised him. She loved this part of her job—sculpting and shaping a person's public profile to maximum effect. She didn't deceive or even stretch the truth; she was just judiciously sparing with what details she shared, very precise with the angle she allowed to be used. If she managed to snag him a feature in one of the country's major newspapers, she would be very careful indeed with how he was presented.

'Tech *wunderkinder* are a dime a dozen,' she informed him. 'So, we need to find another angle. Something a little mysterious, enigmatic, maybe.'

He shook his head. 'But I'm really not enigmatic.'

She laughed. 'You will be. Trust me, Jack. I can

handle this. I'll get back to you in a couple of days with some initial thoughts and ideas.'

Still looking dubious, he murmured his thanks and rose from in front of her desk. When he'd left her office, Lana spun towards the window to gaze unseeingly down at the view of Rockefeller Plaza. She and Christos had been enjoying their new arrangements for almost two weeks. Two weeks tomorrow, in fact, which was why her stomach was tightening with both anticipation and nerves. If, miraculously, she was pregnant on the first try—well, their *many* tries—then she could potentially take a pregnancy test tomorrow. There were a few tests out there that could be taken even sooner, but Lana hadn't wanted to deal with the painful disappointment of a false negative.

When she and Christos had talked about even the possibility of a baby, that little bundle of cells, she'd felt such an ache of longing, it had nearly made her breathless. She wanted this. She wanted it even more now that she knew what married life—*real* married life—with Christos was like.

The last two weeks had, frankly, been incredible. While her days had remained busy with work, her nights had been spent in bed with Christos, discovering delights she had never known existed, learning his body as well as her own in a new and entirely delightful way.

But it wasn't just those sex-soaked nights, Lana knew. It was everything else, too. It was evenings spent on the sofa, answering emails, her feet in

Christos's lap. It was the cup of coffee he handed her when she came downstairs in a rush. It was stepping out of the shower and seeing him wink at her in the mirror or chatting about their workdays over glasses of chilled Chardonnay.

It wasn't, however, anything more than that. It *wasn't* heartfelt conversations, or sharing intimate personal revelations, or saying anything remotely emotional. Yes, Lana could acknowledge that what they did in bed *felt* emotional, or at least intimate. She felt more connected to Christos than to any other human being, ever. But as long as that sense of exposure, a revealing and acceptance of self, stayed in the bedroom, she was fine. *Fine.*

And really, it was all good. She was grateful to Christos for showing her how things could be between a man and a woman when it came to physical intimacy, because when she thought of how Anthony had treated that aspect of a relationship...well, everything in her curdled and cringed with guilt and shame. Sex, for him, had been a way to both dominate and humiliate her. With Christos it had been a shared experience of pleasure, and exploration, and joy.

Yes, she was very grateful to him for teaching her that, over and over again. But not, she thought, of teaching or showing her anything else. Because while she was glad she'd developed in that area, she still wasn't willing to risk her heart. To love someone, to let them in that much, give them the power, not just to humiliate her, as Anthony had done, but to *hurt* her.

Already she sensed Christos could have the power to do that, if she let him, which was why she was standing by her word that she wouldn't. And as long as she held to that line, she'd be fine. Their marriage would be great.

Lana let out a long, slow breath, a smile curving her lips as she turned from the window to get ready for her next meeting.

By six o'clock that evening, she was heading back home with a spring in her step. Amazing how she looked forward to heading back to the house that had always felt, while a haven, an empty one. She'd always liked how she'd been able to let her hair down—literally—and be herself in her own space, but she was starting to realise how much better it was to do that in the company of another person.

Having Christos see and accept her—and even find her sexy and beautiful—in her sweats was far better than simply lounging around in them by herself. It was a discovery that had the power to knock her for six, if she let it. She chose not to. She was gliding on the surface of things, smooth and easy, and she suspected Christos was, too. He certainly hadn't attempted to plumb any emotional depths, far from it. This marriage, as it currently was, suited them both, which was exactly what she wanted. Everything was absolutely great.

So why, sometimes, when she let herself, did she

feel a twinge of unease, a flicker of restlessness? Lana chose not to dwell on it. Gift horses and all that. She just wanted to enjoy what so far had been wonderful…and not think any further than that.

'Hello, beautiful.' Christos greeted her at the door with a kiss and a smile; he had made himself at home in her brownstone, which Lana found she liked. He'd only brought his clothes, laptop, and a few books, and yet even so it was nice to see his things scattered around. She'd asked him if he'd minded leaving his loft apartment in Soho—a soaring space of metalwork and glass—and he'd shrugged and said they could hardly raise a family in two separate abodes.

Well, they could, Lana knew, but it wasn't the way they were choosing to do it. Sometimes she wondered if they were a little crazy, to live this normal-seeming life, without any of the emotional attachments. What if it all blew up in their faces?

'Hello,' she replied, and kicked off her usual stilettos with a groan of satisfaction. 'Good day at work?'

'Fair. Made a million dollars.'

It was a joke they'd shared from way back when, when they'd met infrequently, and Lana had started by asking him that question.

'Only a million?' she quipped, and he shrugged. 'It was a slow day.'

She was on her way to the kitchen when she stopped and saw the serious, expectant look on his face. Her stomach felt as if it were curling in on itself. 'What is it?' she asked uncertainly.

'I bought something for you. Technically, for us, but, you know.'

'No, I don't.' It was amazing how quickly her loose-limbed relaxation could turn into tension, to fear. How quickly she expected everything to start to go wrong. 'What are you talking about?'

'This,' Christos said, and withdrew a slim rectangular box from the pocket of his suit jacket.

Lana stared at in uncomprehendingly for a few seconds before she clocked what it was.

A pregnancy test.

Christos watched the colour drain from Lana's face and wondered if he'd just made a big mistake. It was only a test, that was all, but she was looking at him as if he were trying to hand her a snake.

'Lana?'

'It's not even been two weeks yet.'

Was that all that was bothering her? 'Two weeks from tomorrow, but the test is good from ten days after ovulation. I even read the box.' If he was attempting to raise a smile, he failed. She was staring wide-eyed at the box, her face still pale.

'You really want this,' she stated quietly, almost to herself.

Christos felt a frisson of unease, almost annoyance. 'We both want this, Lana. At least I thought we did.' He blew out a breath. 'I was just trying to be helpful.'

She glanced up at his face, a bit of colour coming

back to her cheeks. 'I know. I'm sorry. It just threw me. I didn't realise you were counting the days.'

Christos frowned. He wouldn't have said he was counting the days, not *exactly*, but… 'Is there a reason I shouldn't have been?'

'No.' But she sounded unsure, and he didn't know why. He felt as if they'd stepped onto shaky ground without him having realised they'd even moved. It was just a pregnancy test, a matter of expediency, to make sure. Wasn't it?

Because he knew once she took that test, there was a chance its result could change everything. 'You don't have to take it now,' he said, although that had been his hope. 'Just keep it for…whenever.'

She glanced up at him, humour lightening her eyes to the colour of sunlight dancing on the sea. 'Really? You're willing to be that patient?'

He smiled back, relief flooding through him. 'Well…'

'I'll do it now, Christos.' She took the box from him. 'I was just freaked out for a second, because… this is real, isn't it?'

'You'll only know when you take the test.'

She shook her head. 'I don't mean that. Whether it's positive or negative this time…this is the choice we've made. The road we've taken.'

He hesitated, because he knew what she meant, and the import she was giving this moment forced him to give it the same. This wasn't just real, it was serious. Somehow, over the last two weeks, he'd been having so much fun that he'd forgotten that this was all for keeps, that there were lives involved, if not hearts. And if Lana really was pregnant with their child…well, the stakes would then be stratospheric.

He might not only be in danger of letting her down, but of letting their *child* down. How had he not considered this properly before? Realised the inherent danger?

Because, he knew, he hadn't wanted to. And he still wanted a baby. A wife. A *family*. He just didn't want to blow it…with any of those people.

'All right,' Lana said with a small, wry smile, although he could tell she was nervous, 'I'll see you in about three minutes.' And she slipped away from him to the bathroom off the hall.

Christos paced the living room, amazed at how three minutes could feel so long. He was so not good at these crucial moments. If Lana came out and she wasn't pregnant, she might be upset. And he wasn't so good at comforting people.

'Christos, please. Come home. I need you.'

He pictured his sister's tearstained face on the screen of his laptop, and how he'd ended the call, unable to cope with her grief, her need. What kind of unfeeling monster was he? And when he thought of what had happened next… Kristina's taut voice on the call, the news that his baby sister was being rushed to the hospital… Christos never wanted to feel that utter hollowing out of his insides, the realisation of just how terribly he had failed someone he loved. His sister had forgiven him; at least she'd said she had. But he'd never forgiven himself.

But he'd do better now, he promised himself. He would. And if Lana *was* pregnant…

His heart flipped over, although whether in hope or sheer terror Christos wasn't quite sure. He really should have thought all this through a lot more, except…

He knew he wouldn't have changed a thing.

The last two weeks had really been that amazing—and not just the nights, which certainly had been mind-blowing and heaven-sent. But the days too, the little moments. When he woke up and Lana was still snuggled in his arms, soft and warm. When he was working and a sudden text popped up, with a funny gif or link from her, making him smile because her sense of humour, although hidden, rivalled his own. When she plopped her feet in his lap with a knowing, shamefaced grin, and he laughingly started to rub her feet.

There was so much he was enjoying about this marriage, and a baby would only make it better. Right?

The door to the bathroom opened, and Christos whirled around. He realised he didn't actually know what he wanted the test result to be—a baby would be great, yes, but having more time together first would be good, too. And he wasn't sure how Lana would feel about it, either. This had all happened so fast, after all; a month ago she hadn't even known she'd been in menopause. She hadn't even thought she'd wanted a baby.

If she wasn't pregnant, maybe it would be better

for them both. Give them a little time to think, to breathe, to be…

'Christos?' Her voice was soft, tentative. She held the test stick in her hand, but he couldn't see its little window—one line or two?

'Did you find out?' Of course she had, but he couldn't tell based on her expression. She looked uncertain, a little afraid, maybe hopeful…

'Is it…?'

'Positive.' She showed him the stick and he saw two pale pink lines. 'I'm pregnant.'

CHAPTER ELEVEN

'I DON'T KNOW about this.'

'It looks great, trust me.' Lana gave Jack Philips a breezily reassuring smile as he dubiously regarded his reflection in the full-length mirror in one of her office's conference rooms. He was trying on different suits for the feature interview she'd bagged him with a major lifestyle magazine. It was a coup for him as well as her, and now he just needed to present the right image—confident, purposeful, assured. The streamlined suit of royal-blue silk was perfect, even if Jack was having his doubts. The glossy image she'd prepared for him was, Lana knew, hard for a fairly shy, geeky guy to step into, but she was confident he could do it…with her help.

Hadn't she done the same thing for herself, when she was just twenty-one, on her own, dirt poor and desperate, on a mission to turn herself into someone glossy and polished and assured? After Anthony had finished with her two years later, she'd been determined to turn herself into the kind of woman who couldn't be hurt, who would stride the world and crush men beneath her heel. She'd wanted to be glossy and hard, distant and strong, and she'd done it. She'd changed herself, at least on the outside if not the inside, because you never could fully escape your past. Still, with the outside she'd succeeded, in spades. So could Jack Philips.

'So,' she asked, her hands on her hips, her eyebrows raised in expectation as she smiled at him. 'What do you think? Does it work?'

'If you say so,' he finally said with a smile. 'Although this isn't something I would normally ever wear.'

'I know.' If he'd been in charge, he'd have shown up to a very important interview in a ragged T-shirt and dirty jeans. But that was why he—and countless others—hired her. To perfect their image, to *create* it, just as she'd done for herself.

Once, that had given Lana a huge sense of satisfaction, of meaning. She knew full well how the longing to be someone different could take over your life, your heart. Only lately, she felt a flicker of—not unease, no, not quite that, but *something.* She was beginning to wonder if she really wanted to change people into something else. If life was really all about the image.

These doubts had started worrying at her ever since Christos had come into her life, her bed, and especially since she'd found out she was pregnant just over a month ago. She'd gone into both those things assuming they wouldn't change who she was, how she acted, what she believed—and yet she was realising more and more how wrong-headed that was. How wrong-hearted. Of course such monumental things would change her. They would have to.

But as for Jack…all they were talking about was a suit.

'So, you're definitely happy with it?' she confirmed, and he nodded, not looking entirely happy but she was pretty sure he could be convinced. The interview wasn't for a few weeks, after all.

After finishing their meeting, Lana went back to her own office, grateful for the mug of ginger tea Michelle had left on her desk. Michelle was the only person besides Christos whom she'd told about her pregnancy; it had been hard to hide, anyway, when the morning sickness had started ten days ago. Michelle had been understanding, not batting an eyelid when Lana had to rapidly excuse herself from a meeting or had a fifteen-minute catnap at her desk.

Christos had been understanding too, and so very sweet. He was always bringing home little treats—saltine crackers from her childhood after she'd mentioned a craving; comfy socks; bubble bath. Anything to make her adjustment to pregnancy easier.

She couldn't fault him at all, Lana thought, and yet…

And yet.

That flicker of unease she'd been doing her best to ignore burned a little higher inside her. It had started when she'd first told Christos she was pregnant. She'd seen how shocked he'd looked, and that hadn't bothered her, because, heaven knew, she'd been shocked herself. She didn't think either of them had been prepared for how quickly she'd become pregnant, especially considering her condition.

He'd hugged her then, and kissed her, and she would have thought everything was absolutely fine, except for the invisible, paper-thin wall that had gone up between them. Lana could not point to a single thing or even a single moment when she'd seen and recognised that wall. She had no evidence, no reason, *and yet*. And yet. She knew it was there. She *felt* it.

It was in the tiny pause Christos sometimes took before he spoke. It was in the way he smiled at her, his eyes crinkling at the corners the way they always did, but she felt as if he were looking at something else, or maybe even inward. It was in the way he took her into his arms, the way he cherished her body, yet still, somehow, holding some essential part of himself back, so she was left completely and wonderfully sated, and yet still somehow feeling empty, wanting more.

She kept telling herself she was being ridiculous, oversensitive and maybe even delusional, and then she'd see him and feel it again, and knew she wasn't. But maybe it wasn't Christos who had changed; it was herself. She was aware of something she hadn't been before, because this pregnancy had changed her, along with being with Christos in this new way. Maybe this was the way Christos had always acted with her and she hadn't known, wouldn't have been bothered if she had known, because that was how she'd been operating, too.

Hold yourself back. Keep your heart, that essential part of yourself, back, so you won't get hurt, give someone the power to hurt you.

That had certainly become her MO since Anthony. Anthony, whom she'd felt as if she'd given everything to, even as she now wondered whether she'd truly loved him at all. She'd believed she had, certainly, and she'd certainly let him hurt her. She'd been so dazzled by the advertising exec ten years her senior who had sought her out, seemed to make her the centre of his world, wined and dined her, a girl from the sticks who had never known glamour or attention or interest. Never mind that he'd humiliated her more times than she could count—mocking her at her most exposed and vulnerable, complaining about her performance in bed, telling her she could never please a man. Studying her like a specimen and then squashing her like a bug. That was what she'd thought love was, but now she knew it wasn't. It wasn't anything like it.

But was this?

The question, over the last few weeks, had become more insistent even as she'd done her best to ignore it. She ignored it now as she got ready to go home, looking forward to a weekend of relaxing with Christos. It was so much simpler to focus on what they did together than how they did—or didn't—feel. Because the truth was, whether it was love or not—and really, love was just a word—Lana was starting to fear that she cared more for Christos than he did for her. *That* was what she was feeling…and she didn't like it, not one bit.

She arrived home just after six, surprised to find Christos had already arrived and changed into casual clothes—chinos and an open-necked shirt in a pale green that made his eyes glint like jade. He was in the kitchen, perusing the cupboards with a frown, when she came through the front door.

'I was thinking of cooking you something,' he told her as she came up the stairs, 'but I realised I'd have no idea what you'd be in the mood for.'

'*I* don't know what I'm in the mood for,' Lana replied with a smile. She wasn't even joking. Since the morning sickness had hit, her food cravings changed by the hour, if not the minute, and sometimes she couldn't manage anything at all. Her OB had told her the symptoms should ease soon, but that morning sickness could be a good sign that the baby was healthy and growing. She'd have her first ultrasound in just under a month, and already she couldn't wait.

'Shall I just order something in?' Christos asked, opening the drawer where they kept all the takeaway menus. He wasn't quite looking at her, hadn't actually looked at her properly since she'd come home, and Lana felt it—but not enough to call him on it. She wouldn't know what to say, and the truth was she wasn't sure she wanted to hear his response.

'Sure, let's order something in,' she said. 'I'll just go change.'

'Before you do…' Christos's voice held a certain

gravitas that she hadn't heard in a long while, and Lana stilled, her heart already starting to thump. Was this the moment he'd tell her that he'd changed his mind, that he didn't want to do this marriage and baby thing any more? She was braced for it, she realised, expecting it even, ready and yet not ready at all.

'Yes?' she asked, hoping her voice sounded light, mildly inquiring.

'One of my sisters has reached out to me,' Christos told her after one of those tiny pauses. 'I haven't told her or any of my family about the pregnancy yet, but it made me realise that I probably should. And that maybe you should meet them. We could go some time in the next few weeks, if you're amenable. We won't see them that often,' he continued rather hurriedly, 'and in fact, I rarely see them as it is. But…considering they'll be this baby's relatives, well.' He shrugged, his gaze sliding away from hers. Again. 'I want our child to know his or her family.'

'So do I,' Lana replied quietly. Especially as she didn't have any family on her side—never having known her father and her mother dead. No siblings, no grandparents, none of that rambunctious and loving extended family that so many people took for granted, Christos, perhaps, included. 'I'd love to meet them, Christos.'

He let out a breath and nodded slowly, almost in resignation. He didn't look as if he was enjoying the prospect of such a meeting, far from it. He looked like a man who had just been told the date of his execution. Why?

She couldn't, Lana knew, ask, although she wished she could. She wished they had that kind of relationship, that kind of trust, but they didn't, and that much had been clear in the last month. They'd had lots of lovely evenings relaxing together, and even lovelier nights in bed. They'd had long, lazy brunches at restaurants in the city, and long, lazy walks through Central Park in the hazy heat of summer. They'd had enjoyable conversations about work, and life in the city, and had exchanged different sections of the newspapers, chatting about what they'd read. They'd shared so much, and yet in moments like this it felt like nothing at all, because they had not shared their hearts. They'd both made sure not to.

Lana had no idea what her husband was truly thinking or feeling in this moment, and she knew she couldn't ask him, wouldn't dare to. That was the agreement they'd made, after all, right at the beginning. No emotion. No soul-baring. No attachment and certainly no love. It wasn't Christos's fault that somehow, against her own better judgment, she was starting to change her mind. Her heart.

It wasn't his fault at all, and she needed to get herself in line *pronto*, because falling in love with someone who had no interest in loving her was definitely *not* on her agenda...and never would be.

'Be back in a few minutes,' she told him lightly, and walked back towards their shared bedroom. Whatever was going on with Christos and his family, she wouldn't ask about it, Lana promised herself. She wouldn't ask about anything, and she'd stop this pointless examination of her own feelings because she didn't *want* to know how she felt—and she certainly didn't want to feel it.

Christos stared out at the road stretching towards the horizon, his gaze on the hazy blue summer sky, his jaw tight. He rolled back his shoulders, which were also tight. He and Lana were driving to his father's house on Long Island, where his three sisters and his father would be joining them. He hadn't seen his father or Kristina, Sophia, and Thalia in longer than he cared to remember. More than months, probably years. He'd let time drift by without ever going home, even though it was only an hour and a half away. It had just always been easier to stay away. To not have to look in his sisters' eyes and see their disappointment, never mind how his father could never even look at him in the eye at all. Everyone tried to hide it, of course, to pretend it wasn't there, but he knew all the same. He *felt* it.

Not that he intended on telling Lana any of that. He'd enjoyed these last few months with her, in large part because they *hadn't* got into all that stuff. They'd skimmed the surface of their emotions while enjoying the pleasure of each other's company—and bodies. The perfect arrangement, exactly what he wanted, so he really had no idea why he was feeling so restless and antsy now.

Probably because he was going back home, a

place that had filled him with only dread and sorrow ever since his mother had died twenty years ago and he'd failed her in the worst way possible.

'Do you know,' Lana said into the silence, and he could tell by her tone she was trying to sound light, even though she wasn't feeling it, 'I don't know anything about your family? That seems strange, now.'

'Why should it seem strange?' he returned, his tone borderline surly. What was *wrong* with him? 'That's how we both agreed it would be. Should be. I don't know your family, either.'

She was quiet for her moment, and when Christos risked a sideways glance, he saw how thoughtful she looked, how opaque her eyes.

'That's true,' she said finally. 'I know your mother died when you were young, and you knew I grew up without a father.' Something he never had asked about, for a *reason*. 'And that's all we know about each other's families.'

He stayed silent, deciding it was less risky than offering some commentary on her observation, which was making him feel uncomfortable for all sorts of complicated reasons.

'Are you willing,' she asked after another frozen pause, 'to at least tell me their names?'

Guilt flashed through him, chased by irritation. She was making him sound as if he'd been unreasonable, and he hadn't been. He'd simply held to their original agreement. She wasn't going back on it, was she? The possibility filled him with both dread and something else he couldn't name.

'Of course I'll tell you their names,' he replied as mildly as he could. 'I have three younger sisters—Kristina is the oldest, then Sophia, then Thalia.'

'Three sisters! I think you might have told me that before, actually,' she replied musingly. 'When we first met. But I must have forgotten.' He shrugged. Sometimes he tried to forget too, but he never did.

'What are they like?'

What were they *like*? Christos felt his throat going tight. Damn it, he did not want to answer these kinds of questions. But it wasn't particularly unreasonable, he told himself, for Lana to ask them. It wasn't even emotional. It was just that he was feeling pretty raw, now that he was going home, and now that Lana was carrying his own child.

When she'd first told him she was pregnant—a mere three weeks after her initial proposal!—he'd been thrilled. For a millisecond. Following that, he'd been completely terrified, and tried to hide it ever since.

What on earth had made him think he could have a kid without screwing it up? Disappointing and even failing him or her, the way he had his own family? Not that he ever wanted to explain any of that to Lana. And so, he'd been living in this state of paralysis—enjoying their time together, as they had been before she'd taken that test, trying to be as thoughtful and considerate as he could be, without it actually costing him anything. Without thinking about the future.

'What are they like?' he repeated, mainly to stall

for time. He wasn't used to talking about his family, or even thinking about them, not if he could help it. 'Kristina is a busybody, if a well-meaning one. That's what she'd call herself, anyway. Always wanting to know about you, always willing to listen.' Even when he refused to talk. 'She'll ask you a million questions the minute you arrive, so consider this fair warning.'

'I will,' Lana replied, a smile in her voice.

Against all odds and expectations, Christos found himself relaxing. A little.

'Sophia is completely different. She's very focused and direct, but she can also be very private.' After their mother had died, he and Sophia had been similar in their silent grief, unable to connect with anyone, shutting down rather than engaging with the people who loved them most.

'And Thalia?'

'Thalia…' The name escaped him on a sigh. The baby of the family, full of laughter and light…until she hadn't been. And Christos hadn't been there for her, even though she'd asked him. *Begged* him. He'd refused her…with disastrous consequences. 'She's… emotional,' he said at last, and he saw Lana raise her eyebrows. 'When she's happy, she's buzzing and the best to be around, and when she's not…' He trailed off, remembering when she most certainly had not been.

'Help me, Christos.'

'I can't.'

'Christos?' Lana asked softly, and he shook his head to expel the memory.

'That's it.'

'What about your father?'

His father. Christos would have closed his eyes if he hadn't been driving. 'My father loved my mother very much,' he said after a moment. 'And when she died, it was like the life had gone out of him. The… essence.'

'I depend on you, Christos. You're the man of the family now. You have to take care of your sisters.'

Except he hadn't.

'That must have been very hard,' Lana said quietly.

'Yes.' The word was quiet, but Christos heard how heartfelt he sounded. It hadn't been hard; it had been near impossible. Agony, every day, and then worse after, until he'd finally left them all behind, tried to find some freedom, some peace, and thought he hadn't, fooled himself, really, because he knew he never had. Not if he was feeling this way now.

To his surprise, Lana reached over and rested her hand on his thigh, a gesture of comfort, one he hadn't expected. Although they'd certainly been affectionate—and more—with each other in the last few months, they hadn't offered each other *comfort*. Not like this—something quiet and tender and heartfelt.

He had an urge to shrug her hand off, tell her it wasn't needed, and just as strong an urge to grab hold of it and press it to his cheek. He did neither. He just kept driving, his jaw tight, his gaze on the road.

An hour later they were pulling up to the sprawling colonial in one of Brookhaven's gracious streets, the only home he'd known before he'd moved to New York. His father, Niko Diakos, had started life in a tenement on the Lower East Side, worked his way up in the banking business until middle management had allowed him the trappings of respectability. He'd never made the millions Christos had, first with the apps he'd developed and then with more advanced technological investments, but he'd had a solid business, a solid life.

Until his beloved wife Marina had died. Even now, as Christos parked in the driveway, he was picturing the day his mother's body was taken from the house—a sheet to cover her, so Christos hadn't been able to see her face. His father weeping, his sisters huddled together on the stairs. In his memory, that day was dark and grey and stormy, but he knew in reality it had been a sunny summer's day much like this one. Funny, how he couldn't remember the sun shining. Only the terrible, vast numbness he'd felt inside, as if a frozen tundra had claimed him, covered him in snow and ice.

'Christos...should we go in?'

Christos glanced at Lana, who was looking troubled and all too sympathetic, as if she knew how painful these memories were, how hard he tried never to think about them. But she didn't know, he reminded himself, because he'd never told her…and he never would.

'Yes.' He forced the corners of his mouth up in something like a smile. 'Let's go.'

CHAPTER TWELVE

LANA HAD NO idea what to expect as she walked into the foyer of Christos's family home. Based on what he'd said, and really, what he hadn't said, she'd been braced for a frosty welcome, or at least a formal one. Christos clearly had become alienated from his family—after his mother's death? Or later? And why?

What Lana hadn't expected was for one of his sisters to bustle right up to her, her face lit up with a smile, place her hands on either side of her face and give Lana a smacking kiss on each cheek before enveloping her in a bear hug.

Lana submitted to the hug for a second, completely frozen, utterly shocked, before she managed to put her arms around the unknown sister, although she was already suspecting it was Kristina.

'Finally, he brings you!' Kristina exclaimed. She had a strong Long Island accent and was short and round and full of good humour. Lana liked her instantly. Kristina turned to Christos and shook her finger at him. 'What on earth were you hiding her for? She's gorgeous.'

'I wasn't hiding her,' Christos replied mildly. He seemed like his usual laid-back self, his smile wry, his stance relaxed, but Lana sensed some dark emotion pulsing underneath. Was Christos's image—that rueful, smiling, joking entrepreneur—as much of a façade as hers was, that cool, glossy remote persona she donned like armour? Had they both been pretending all along?

It was a surprising and, she realised, actually welcome thought. She wanted there to be more to Christos in the same way there was more to her—and she wanted them to know that about each other.

Now *that* was not an entirely welcome thought. At least, it was a scary one. She'd never wanted to be known before. She'd made sure she wouldn't be. And yet here she was, thinking she wanted to be known—and more—by Christos?

'Come into the kitchen,' Kristina said, taking her by the hand. 'We've got food—so much food!—and coffee. I want to hear all about you. Every single thing.'

Well, Lana thought wryly as she let herself be led into the heart of the house, if she wasn't going to be known by Christos, she certainly was by his sister.

The rest of his sisters were waiting in the kitchen, Sophia dressed in a tailored blouse and trousers, her smile warm but cautious, while Thalia—because it had to be Thalia—catapulted across the room in a cloud of dark hair and threw her arms around Christos with a squeal.

Christos had to take a step back for balance as he

hugged his sisters back. Lana couldn't see his face, but she had the sense he hadn't been expecting this.

'Why haven't you come home before now?' Thalia exclaimed, her face pressed into his shoulder. She was small and slender, dressed in a pair of oversized dungarees and a T-shirt. 'It's been years, Christos. *Years.*'

'I've been busy,' he replied as he released Thalia. 'But I'm sorry. I should have come home sooner.'

'Yes, you should have.' She wagged a finger at him, seeming playful, but Lana could tell how hurt she was by his absence; her large green eyes were glassy, and her lower lip trembled. She couldn't be much more than twenty, Lana thought, much younger than she'd expected. Kristina and Sophia both looked to be in their early thirties.

'Ah, the prodigal son returns.' A man stepped into the room, looking so much like Christos that Lana thought she knew what her husband would look like in thirty years. He had the same long, lanky frame, although a little less muscular, and his shoulders were slightly stooped. His head of thick, wavy hair was liberally peppered with grey, and there were deep creases by his hazel eyes and from nose to mouth. He smiled at Christos, and Christos gave a jerky nod back, not quite looking at him. The older man's welcoming smile drooped along with his shoulders, and then he straightened and turned to Lana with another warm smile.

'I've been so looking forward to meeting you.'

Lana glanced at Christos, because she realised

she'd never asked him if he'd told his family about their original arrangement, or their newer one. What did they know about the state of Christos's marriage?

'And I've been looking forward to meeting you,' she replied, shaking his hand. 'All of you. Christos has told me about you, so I think I know who you all are. Kristina?' She glanced at the first sister she'd met, who laughed and clapped her hands. 'And Sophia?' Sophia smiled and nodded. 'And Thalia!'

Thalia nodded, without the smile, and Lana felt a flicker of trepidation. The young woman was looking as if she did not welcome her entry into her brother's life.

'Come sit down, sit down,' Kristina said. 'And tell us everything. To think, Christos has been married to you for three whole years and never brought you home.'

So, they did know, Lana realised, but how much?

'We're here now,' Christos said, and his tone was just short of brusque, although it didn't seem to put off Kristina.

'So you are, so you are,' she agreed as they all sat down in the adjoining family room, which was comfortable and welcoming, scattered with sofas of cream leather. 'And we're very glad of it. We've been so curious about the woman who managed to get you to the altar, when there hasn't been another who has been able to get you to a third date!' Lana smiled a little at that, and Kristina nodded knowingly. 'He doesn't tell us himself, of course, but Thalia reads all the articles about him in the gossip or business magazines. She even has a scrapbook!'

Which seemed slightly obsessive, Lana thought, but she supposed understandable, especially if Christos never came home…and why not? Right now, his absence from their lives felt like a mystery. His family was showing nothing but love for him, and meanwhile he was sitting on the sofa next to her, looking relaxed, yes, but she could feel the tension emanating from him like a force field. He did not want to be here, she realised. At all. And she had no idea why.

She didn't get any more clues to the answer to that question as they sat and chatted for the next hour, while Kristina plied them with coffee and Greek pastries. She learned that Kristina lived nearby and ran her own bakery in Brookhaven, while Sophia worked remotely for a graphic design company and had a town house in Long Island City, which shocked Lana, because it was only a twenty-minute subway ride from where she and Christos lived. Why had they never had Sophia over? Why had Christos never met up with her in Manhattan?

Thalia, she learned, lived at home with her father Niko, who had retired from banking ten years ago. She was studying online for a degree in art, but Lana got the sense that she wasn't very interested in her studies. She was twenty-two but she seemed younger, losing interest in the conversation, interrupting people, teasing Christos and then pouting if he didn't reply right away. Lana found her somewhat exhausting, although she tried not to show it. Christos humoured her, but she could tell he found it hard.

Something about Thalia caused him pain, she realised; she sensed it, with an instinct she hadn't possessed until recently. She used to never know what Christos was thinking; now she sensed what he was feeling…but she still didn't understand why.

'She's lovely, Christos.'

Christos stiffened as he turned around from the deck railing where he'd been gazing unseeingly out at the yard, mainly to avoid his family after an intense couple of hours. They'd chatted over coffee and cake and every moment had felt like torture. Thalia's endless needs and demands. Sophia's quiet censure. Kristina's determination to make everything seem normal. His father's sorrowful silence.

He couldn't take any of it, not any of it, not when guilt still ate him up every time he came home.

'Christos?' Kristina's voice was gentle as she came out onto the deck, closing the sliding glass door behind her. 'Why did you never bring her home before?'

He shrugged, not looking at her, as usual. 'I don't come home very often, Kristina. You know that.'

'Yes.' She sighed heavily. 'I know.'

'It's better if I'm not here. I set Thalia off. I make Dad remember.'

'We want you here, Christos,' Kristina said quietly, although he noticed she didn't deny what he'd said. How could she? They both knew it was true.

Ever since their mother had died, he'd failed his family. He hadn't been there when they'd needed him, when Thalia had *begged* him, and had ended up in a psychiatric ward for three months on suicide watch. That was *his* fault, nobody else's.

Yes, it was better for everyone if he stayed away.

'Tell me about Lana,' Kristina said, and Christos shrugged, unable to keep himself from sounding and feeling defensive. He'd never told his family about Lana; they'd found out from the ridiculous society pages. When Thalia had sent him a text, a few months after he and Lana had embarked on their paper marriage, asking him if he was really married, he'd said yes, because he'd had to, but he'd tried to frame it as more of a business merger than a meeting of minds or hearts, because that was what it had been.

As for what it was now…

'She seems softer than I expected,' Kristian ventured when he hadn't said anything. 'From what little you told us, I thought perhaps she was one of those hard-as-nails businesswomen.'

'She is,' Christos replied, 'in the office. She built up her own business from nothing and is one of the most successful PR people in the whole city.' He realised he sounded proud; he *was* proud. Lana's determination and drive were incredible, just one of the many things he—he *liked* about her. Yes.

'Well, she doesn't look hard as nails to me now,' Kristina said with a hint of a smile in her voice. 'She looks like she absolutely adores you.'

What? Christos turned to face his sister, who was smiling affectionately at him, clearly so pleased by this development…except of course it couldn't be true.

'Why do you say that?' he asked, his voice roughening.

'Because it's obvious. The look in her eyes…it's so tender. Besides, a woman knows, Christos.' She shook her head, still smiling. 'I wish I had a man to look at that way. And I wish a man would look at *me* that way.'

'What are you saying?' He realised he sounded almost panicked, and his sister noticed.

'Usually, a man doesn't mind knowing his wife is in love with him,' she remarked. 'Or that he is in love with her. Unless I'm missing something?'

'It's just…' Christos blew out a breath. 'Lana and I are more friends than…' How to finish that sentence?

'Husband and wife?' Kristina guessed. 'Because you looked like husband and wife to me.'

And they hadn't yet told his family about the baby. That was certainly very husband and wife territory.

'It's complicated,' he told his sister.

'Maybe,' she allowed, 'but maybe it doesn't need to be.' He had no idea how to answer that, so he didn't say anything, and his sister continued gently, 'Can't you leave the past where it belongs, Christos, instead of raking it up every time you go home? I know you do—I see it in your eyes, the torment that doesn't need to be there. It happened. It's over. We all want to move on. We're all trying to, except you.'

Christos found he couldn't speak now; his throat was too tight. He just shook his head, averting his face, and Kristina sighed.

'Come inside at least,' she said. 'For supper.'

Christos waited until she'd gone inside, needing a moment alone to compose himself. He took a few deep breaths as he gazed out at the lawn, twilit shadows now lengthening along it. Kristina had to be wrong, he thought. Lana didn't *adore* him. If anything, she'd been more insistent about the no-love clause of their paper marriage, right from the beginning. He was the one who'd fooled himself into thinking he was more open about it all, when he now knew he wasn't. He couldn't be.

And yet…what did he actually *want*? If he put aside his fear of hurting Lana, disappointing her and their child, having to live with that disappointment day after day…did he want to love her? Could he? Could she love him, if she knew the truth about what he'd done, and, more importantly, what he *hadn't* done?

A heaviness settled inside him, because he knew the answer. He couldn't. She couldn't. He would disappoint her, eventually, and she would never love him if she knew how badly he'd let people down. People who had counted on him, and needed him, and loved him.

So, what on earth were they doing, having a baby together, especially if what Kristina had said was true, and Lana had somehow fallen in love with him?

What could that possibly mean for their future?

'Christos,' Sophia called, 'come inside before it gets cold!'

Slowly, his heart leaden inside him, Christos walked inside. Everyone was gathered around the dining-room table, which was laden with food, because, he knew, food was love, especially to a Greek woman.

He found himself seeking out Lana instinctively, and as he caught sight of her across the room, he saw she was looking at him in concern, a small, inquiring smile curving her mouth. There was a new lushness to her body, now she was pregnant, and the morning sickness had started to abate. The tiniest of curves to that reed-thin waist, a fullness to her breasts, her body ripe with his child… It filled him with an emotion he wasn't willing to name.

He managed a smile back, and then decided they might as well get giving the news over with.

'Before we eat,' he announced, not quite looking at anyone, 'Lana and I have something to say.' In his peripheral vision, he saw her eyes widen and he wondered if he should have done this differently—hand in hand, perhaps, with beaming smiles. He had, he realised, sounded rather grim about it all.

'What is it, Christos?' Thalia asked, already impatient.

'Lana is expecting,' he said, trying to inject some enthusiasm into his voice. 'A baby. She's due in February.'

A shocked silence followed this announcement and then Kristina clapped her hands and went to hug him, and then Lana, peppering her with questions about how she was feeling, whether she'd tried ginger tea for morning sickness.

Sophia smiled faintly and gave him a quick kiss on the cheek. 'Don't look so terrified,' she murmured as she stepped back. 'It will all be okay.'

'I'm fine,' Christos replied. His middle sister had always understood him the best, and yet he'd pushed her away too, simply because it had been easier. What had once felt like the right thing to do suddenly seemed selfish. Had Sophia been hurt by his distance? She'd always seemed so self-contained, needing no one, but maybe that was as much of a coping mechanism as any of their other reactions to their mother's death had been. Maybe he should have reached out...and yet he couldn't have. It hadn't felt physically possible.

Another way in which he'd failed.

'I can't believe you're going to be a dad,' Thalia said, not sounding entirely pleased about it, and Christos understood why. She had always been the baby of the family, the surprise blessing, only two years old when his mother had died. She'd never managed to truly grow up, and he suspected she was worried about being replaced.

And yet what was there to replace? He hardly ever saw his baby sister. The best he offered was the occasional hurried text. Another way in which he thought he'd been protecting his family but now just felt selfish.

What was wrong with him? Why was he thinking this way?

This was what coming home did to him. It made him doubt himself, his perception of the past, of his family and how they felt. And that made him start to wonder about other things…like Lana.

Did she really love him? Could she, if she knew what he'd done?

Did he even want answers to those questions?

CHAPTER THIRTEEN

CHRISTOS WAS QUIET on the way home, quieter even than he'd been on the journey there, his jaw tight, his brow furrowed as he gazed out at the road. He seemed deep in thought, and Lana found she didn't want to disturb him.

The day had been wonderful in many ways—Sophia and Kristina both warmly welcoming, his father kindly and gentle, the conversation easy with more laughter than Lana had expected. In some ways, Christos's family felt like the family she had never had…big and noisy, warm and loving, yet Christos didn't seem to appreciate or enjoy any of it at all. And Thalia, Lana acknowledged, had been chilly at best, sometimes even rude, ignoring her in a way that felt pointed, or turning away when she had asked a question.

As for Christos… Lana hadn't missed how positively grim he had sounded when he'd made the announcement about her pregnancy. Was he having second thoughts about everything? Did he not want their baby any more? Did he not want *her*?

She wasn't brave enough to ask him. A few weeks ago, she'd given herself a strict talking-to, to get her feelings in line and stop wondering if she could fall in love with Christos. She wanted to enjoy what they had, and while that felt easy enough because what they had was wonderful, she knew she still felt empty inside. Still wanted more…more than she'd ever let herself want before. And the more she wanted, it seemed the more Christos didn't.

Which was exactly the kind of situation she'd been desperate to avoid. But how did you avoid it, when you didn't have control over your own wayward heart?

It was a conundrum that depressed her, even as she couldn't keep from feeling a contrary flicker of hope that somehow, *somehow* it would all work out. Although there wasn't much room for encouragement with Christos looking so grim as they drove in silence.

Neither of them spoke all the way home, parking the car in the private garage down the street before walking in the summery darkness, the air warm and as soft as velvet. Lana unlocked the door to the brownstone and stepped inside, stopping in surprise when she felt Christos move right behind her. She half turned to him in query, only to have his hands come to her shoulders and he backed her against the wall, just as he had on what had felt like their wedding night. He kissed her then, long and deep, with a tenderness that felt deeper than mere passion, a need that was far more than simple lust.

Surprised, because since she'd become pregnant, Christos had always made sure she initiated their lovemaking, wanting to be considering of her fatigue and tiredness, she stilled and so did he, like a question.

And, acting on instinct, Lana answered it, wrapping her arms around him, drawing her closer to him as their kiss continued, a quiet, heartfelt desperation to it that felt as if it could be her entire undoing. Christos moved his lips to her cheek, and then her neck, and then the hollow of her throat. As he did so, a sound escaped him, something more than a gasp but not quite a sob.

Lana slid her hands to his face, tried to tilt it up towards her. 'Christos,' she whispered. 'Look at me.'

But he wouldn't. He just kept kissing her, her throat, her shoulder, the swell of her breasts above her dress, each brush of his lips so exquisitely tender it brought tears to her eyes. And Lana decided that it was enough. He needed her now, she knew with a bone-deep certainty, not just physically, but emotionally. Even if he would never admit it. Even if he couldn't look her in the eye.

And if he needed her that way, Lana knew unequivocally that she wanted to be needed. She wanted to give herself, all of herself, in a way she never had before. And so, she wrapped her arms around him again and opened her body and even her heart to him as he continued to kiss her, stopping only to draw the sundress she'd been wearing over her head and toss it aside.

Lana knew her body looked different than it had even a mere few weeks ago—her breasts were fuller, her belly gently rounded. Christos cupped her belly with his hands, spreading his fingers wide, before he dropped to his knees and kissed her tiny barely there bump with something close to reverence. Pleasure and something far deeper fired through Lana—in all the months they'd been together as man and wife, she'd never felt closer to him than she did now…and yet still so far away.

She had no idea what he was thinking, or even feeling, but she told herself that knowing he needed her was enough. She would let it be enough.

Christos skimmed his hands down the sides of her belly and then tugged her underwear down, his fingers leaving trails of fire wherever they brushed her skin. Something between a gasp and a shudder escaped Lana as she kicked her underwear aside and Christos pressed his mouth to the centre of her, anchoring her with his hands on her hips, lavishing her with tender love and attention in a way that felt wonderfully, agonisingly intimate. She'd never felt so exposed…or so known. It was as frightening as it was wondrous, and she knew she wouldn't exchange it for the safe, sterile world she'd once known. Not in a million years.

A moan escaped her as her hips arched towards him and he continued his loving ministrations, knowing every slick crevice and fold of the most intimate part of her body. She felt a climax building inside her, like a tidal wave poised to crash over her, pull her into its sensuous, swirling undertow, and something in her instinctively resisted it, because she wanted to share this moment with Christos, and yet as he continued, his mouth moving over her with tender insistence, she knew she couldn't.

The pleasure was too intense, too wonderful, and Christos too determined. She drove her fingers through his hair, her hips pushing against his mouth as a jagged cry escaped her and her body went liquid.

She sagged against the wall, held up only by Christos's hands, her own still fisted in his hair. She was reeling with the aftershocks of her climax when he scooped her up in his arms and carried her to their bed. Lana lay sprawled on it, still dazed, her lips swollen, her body flooded with both pleasure and desire.

Christos stood at the foot of the bed, his face flushed, his eyes glittering and his breath coming fast. He stripped off quickly, tossing his clothes aside with an urgent carelessness, before he joined her on the bed, stretching on top of her, braced on his forearms.

She tried to look him in the eye, but he buried his face in her shoulder as he entered her in one smooth, fluid stroke. Lana wrapped her arms around him, her legs around his waist as she accepted him fully, pulling him more deeply inside her, offering him everything she had to give.

And he received it, clutching her to him as they moved in union, stroke after stroke, the most intimate language ever spoken, needing no words.

When his climax came, hers immediately following, Lana knew she had never felt so entirely united with another person, as one flesh, one mind, one heart. She held him to her, her body still wrapped around his, their bodies shuddering in the aftermath. She wanted to say something, but she was afraid to break the spell that had wrapped around them like a bubble, as fragile as glass.

And the words that hovered on her lips felt too precious and sacred to say, to offer, when she wasn't at all sure what Christos's response would be.

And yet she felt them, burning inside her, needing to be said, and knowing the truth of them with a certainty that both shocked and settled her, because she wasn't afraid. Not any more. No matter what happened.

I love you.

She mouthed the words silently as she held Christos in her arms and felt them reverberate through every fibre of her being.

I love you, Christos. I love you.

Lana closed her eyes and smiled as she held the man who held her heart without even knowing he did.

Christos sat slumped in a chair on the little balcony terrace outside the living room. Below him the street was quiet, the city having finally fallen asleep…unlike him.

Lana had fallen into a doze after their lovemaking, without either of them saying a word, and while she'd slept, curled up on her side, he'd slipped away, pouring himself a generous measure of whisky and bringing it out here, to the dark night, hoping the peace and quiet, the air soft and sultry, would help settle his mind.

He'd been out here an hour and, so far, it wasn't working. He didn't know how he felt, or, at least, he didn't want to think too much about how he felt—and yet at the same time it was consuming him.

Kristina telling him that Lana adored him. The knowledge that these last few months had been the sweetest he'd ever known, and yet he still wanted more. The fear—the terror—that if he told Lana the truth about himself and his failures, she would leave him in a heartbeat. The even greater fear that he would disappoint her or their baby, let them down the way he had so many others.

It was too much to feel. He closed his eyes as he tossed back a burning swallow of whisky.

'Can't sleep?'

Lana's soft voice had Christos tensing in his seat. How had he not heard her come to the doorway? He glanced behind him and saw her standing there like a lovely apparition, swathed in a dressing gown of cream silk, her strawberry-blonde hair tumbled in silken waves about her shoulders.

'No,' he said briefly, and she slipped through the doorway and perched on the chair opposite him. They'd enjoyed many meals out on this terrace, casual conversations, easy laughter.

This wasn't any of those. Already, before she'd

said a word, he was bracing himself, knowing what was coming next.

'Talk to me, Christos,' Lana said softly.

He knew, of course, what she meant, and he wasn't going to be so pathetic as to prevaricate or pretend he didn't. He'd always been determined, right from the beginning, to be honest, to be fair, to be kind. He just hadn't realised how hard it would become.

Christos gazed into the amber depths of his glass. 'What do you want me to tell you?' he asked heavily.

'What you're thinking right now would be a good start.'

A sigh escaped him, and he raked a hand through his hair. 'I don't even know, Lana, and that's the truth of it.'

'Why was it so hard to go home?' she asked. 'And why do you go home so rarely?'

'Because it's so hard.'

'Why, though?'

Christos closed his eyes briefly, knowing he was going to tell her and yet dreading it all the same. But maybe it was better she knew. It would, he suspected, keep her from falling any more in love with him, and maybe that was what they both needed—a reminder of how it was supposed to be between them.

'Christos…?'

'It's hard because every time I come home, I'm reminded of how I disappointed and failed my family, back when my mother died. It's hard on me, but it's also hard on them. Seeing me stirs up my father's grief, Thalia's issues.' He glanced at her. 'I presume you saw how high strung and emotionally fragile she seemed at times?'

Lana's expression was both thoughtful and sombre, her head tilted to one side. 'Yes, I did.'

'That's because of me.'

Lana was silent for a moment. 'Surely it can't entirely be down to you, Christos,' she said finally, her voice quiet but holding a certain firm reasonableness. 'You're not the only thing in her life. There have to be other issues affecting her mental health.'

'Maybe, but I trigger them. I know I do, because I caused them at the start.'

Again, Lana was silent, absorbing what he said. He didn't feel any condemnation from her, not yet, but he certainly felt it in himself. He always did when he remembered that agonisingly painful time.

'Tell me,' she said finally, 'what happened when your mother died.'

As she said the words, Christos realised, with a pang of shocked relief, that he actually *wanted* to tell her. He wanted to let it go, and, moreover, he wanted her to know about it. How it might change things between them he had no idea, only that it would, perhaps irrevocably, but it needed to be said.

'My mother was diagnosed with cancer when I was fourteen,' he began slowly, choosing his words with care, each one feeling laborious, laid down like an offering. 'It was difficult. Thalia was only a baby, Kristina twelve and Sophia ten. My father was loving, but he worked all the time and he struggled to cope with the demands…not just physically, but emotionally. I wanted to be there for him, for them all, but it was hard.'

'I'm sure it was,' Lana murmured, her voice soft with compassion.

'At first my mother tried to go on as normal. She wouldn't talk about her chemotherapy, or how sick she was, and she was always there to greet us with a smile.' Already he felt his throat thickening. 'She was so strong, and I suppose that's why it came as a shock when suddenly she wasn't. When I was sixteen, she stopped treatment. There had been a few months of seeming remission, and I think we were all hopeful. Then the cancer came back, as it often does, more aggressive than ever before. She wanted to go into a hospice, but my father insisted she come home. He wanted to be with her. He loved her very, very much.' His voice almost broke and he drew a quick, steadying breath.

Seeing his father absolutely overcome with grief, barely able to function as his mother had withered away, had cemented in him a certainty that he never wanted to love someone that much. Need them so desperately.

Yet what if you already do?

Christos pushed that thought aside. 'Those weeks she was at home were awful,' he said quietly. 'She was so weak, so…different. And we had no help, because my father didn't want anyone to see her like that. He wanted everyone to remember my mother as she used to be—a laughing, lovely, beautiful woman. And she wasn't any more. I didn't even like seeing her…she'd lost so much weight, and her face looked…it looked like a skull.' He pictured her eyes, burning into him, begging him. 'In all truth, I could barely stand to sit with her.' He bowed his head, the words coming faster now, the confession like a bloodletting. 'And so, I wouldn't. I avoided her, and she knew I was, and I know it hurt her. Kristina and Sophia could both handle it, they sat with her for hours. Kristina would come in with Thalia, who was just two, put her in my mother's arms, and help her to hold her. And I… I stayed away.'

'That's understandable, Christos,' Lana said quietly, and he let out a hard, almost wild laugh.

'Is it? Is it understandable that the day before she died, she asked me to sit with her? She knew she was dying, that she would die soon. *I* knew she would die soon. Her strength was seeping away…you could practically see it happening, minute by minute. She begged me, Lana. *Begged* me, with tears in her eyes, her voice. "Please, Christos, let me see you. Let me hug you and say goodbye to you." And you know what I did?' He drew another breath, his voice turning jagged with pain. 'I pretended I hadn't heard her. I walked right by her bedroom—she was sitting up in bed, even though she had no strength, her arms outstretched to me, calling. And I didn't go in. I didn't even answer her. I never saw her again. She died that night.' He dropped his head into his hands as a shudder ripped through him, and then, in surprise, he felt Lana's arms, soft and accepting, fold around him.

'Oh, Christos.' Her voice was soft, sad, and so

very tender. *'Christos.'* As she held him, he felt the sobs building in his chest and he wanted to keep them there. He *needed* to, and yet he couldn't. He couldn't, and they escaped him in choked gasps as she held him and he cried for the mother he'd disappointed, the mistakes he'd made, the grief he'd repressed, the regret that had been eating away at him for two decades.

'I'm sorry,' he finally managed, wiping his eyes, half ashamed, half relieved by his emotional display, the kind of histrionics he'd never let himself indulge in, ever. Yet here he was.

'Don't be sorry.' She pressed her hand against his damp cheek, looking fiercely into his eyes. 'Never be sorry, Christos, for showing me your heart.'

The words pierced him like a sword. His heart? Yes, he had, but…but it went against their agreements, their instincts. 'Lana…'

'Don't say anything,' she said quietly, briefly laying a finger against his lips. 'I know it's not what we agreed. And it may not be what you want—'

'I don't know what I want,' he admitted in a low voice. 'Not any more.'

'Then don't say anything,' she said again, her voice fierce and determined. 'Let's just be.' She pressed a kiss to his lips, and he clasped the back of her head, holding her to him, needing her more than ever.

'There's more I haven't told you,' he confessed when they had broken apart. Now that he'd begun, he wanted to say all of it. 'It wasn't just that one time. I failed in so many ways…after my mother's death, my father asked me to be there for my sisters, because he was so broken by grief, and I wasn't. I *wasn't.* I ignored them, I got irritated by them, I shut down in every way possible.'

He searched her face for signs of disappointment, of judgment, but found none. 'And then that just became the way I operated, and they accepted it, but I always saw their disappointment. My father, too… he's never been able to look me in the eye since my mother died. He's more disappointed than angry, but that feels worse.' He drew a breath, gazing straight at her, seeing only empathy. 'When I left for university at eighteen, I was glad to get away. I tried to come back as little as possible, even though it added to Kristina and Sophia's burdens, especially with Thalia being so little…for some reason, she'd latched onto me, the big brother, and made me a role model when I was anything but.' He paused, steeling himself for what came next.

'When she was fifteen, she had her first depressive episode. She called me, begged me to come see her. She was in such a state, crying, pleading…and it reminded me of my mother. Of her begging me to sit with her. And I couldn't… I just couldn't…' He stopped, composed himself, and started again. 'So, I told her no. I texted Kristina, to tell her to look after her, but I didn't answer any of Thalia's other messages. I turned off my phone and acted like it hadn't happened. That night…' His voice choked again. 'That night Thalia tried to kill herself—cut her wrists, almost bled out. It was touch and go for days, but thankfully she survived. She spent three months in a secure psychiatric unit, on suicide watch. That was my fault, Lana. All my fault. And you can't tell me I was young, that I can be forgiven, because I wasn't. I was nearly *thirty*. It was only three years before I met you.' He stopped then, waited for the judgment that would surely come.

'And you've clearly been paying for it ever since,' Lana told him quietly. She didn't sound condemning, but her voice was firm and level. 'I can see that full well, Christos, and I won't excuse what you did, because it *was* wrong. It was a terrible mistake. But how long must you pay for your sins? Will you ever forgive yourself? Will you allow yourself to be forgiven?'

He shook his head. 'My family doesn't forgive me.'

'I'm not sure about that,' Lana replied. 'But I know you don't forgive yourself.'

'And you think I should?' He couldn't keep from sounding incredulous.

'What benefit is there in raking yourself over the coals for it, again and again?' she challenged quietly. 'After a certain point, regret isn't helpful. It just festers like a wound, like a poison. Torturing yourself with guilt doesn't help you. It doesn't help your family. And it won't help our family.' She took his hand and pressed it to her middle. 'Our baby needs a father who isn't wracked with guilt, determined to be distant in case he messes up. He or she needs a dad who is there, who is involved and invested and fully present. You can be that father, Christos. I know you can.'

He stared at her, desperately wanting to believe her, and yet also so afraid to. He'd already failed too many times. Even if he could forgive himself for that—and with Lana's help, maybe he could—he knew he would not be able to forgive himself if he let down Lana and their child. Never.

And with his track record, it felt as if it was only a matter of time.

'Christos?' Lana prompted softly, and because he couldn't tell her all that, he simply took her in his arms. She came willingly, wrapping herself around him, her cheek tucked into his chest, and Christos closed his eyes, letting himself savour the moment, because heaven only knew what the future held.

CHAPTER FOURTEEN

'I FEEL LIKE a monkey in dressing-up clothes.'

Jack Philips was staring at Lana, dressed in his narrow-legged royal-blue silk suit, looking dapper and handsome and very unhappy.

Lana rested one hand on her burgeoning baby bump. It was November, the ochre and russet leaves fluttering from the trees in Central Park, the air holding a decided crisp chilliness. She was twenty-six weeks along and she was *finally* blooming. After the morning sickness had abated and her bump had begun to show, she'd felt an unequivocal excitement for this next stage of life.

That, she acknowledged wryly, had maybe less to do with her burgeoning bump and more to do with her relationship with Christos. Since that night on the terrace, when he'd shared so much of his story, his heart, their relationship had grown both stronger and deeper. They hadn't said it in words, but Lana had felt it. The emotion. The *love*. Admittedly, those three little words hadn't crossed either of their lips, and Lana tried not to wonder or worry about why not. She wanted to be content with what they had, reminding herself of what Michelle had said—*'That sounds a lot like love to me.'*

Did it really matter if they hadn't said the words? If they never did, even? Lana knew she felt them every day, and she hoped, she *hoped* Christos did, too.

But right now, she needed to think of Jack. His interview had been bumped several times, but the photographer and journalist were now coming to her office in just fifteen minutes, and Jack looked great…but also not so great.

Lana was well used to last-minutes jitters from her clients, whether they were about to give an interview, or a speech or host a party. Part of her job was talking them down, building them up. Giving them that shot in the arm of confidence that helped them step into the image she'd created for them.

But right now, she realised she wasn't sure she wanted to do that. If Jack was unhappy with his look, the lacquer of sophistication she'd painted on him with smart clothes and styled hair, chunky glasses, and a practised script, why bother with it at all? For ten years she'd been all about the gloss, but in the last few months it had started to flake away, and she hadn't even minded.

She'd started wearing her hair in its natural waves rather than straightened to a gleaming sheet, and she'd worn less make-up, too. Power suits didn't go well with pregnancy and so she'd had to make do with tailored maternity dresses. All in all, her look was softer, and she felt softer, as well as more approachable, more herself. Her real self, the self she'd hidden when she'd walked away from a broken relationship, determined to be different, because that had to be what people wanted, since Anthony certainly hadn't wanted the real her.

But Christos seemed to.

If she could trust it and not question anything. Live in the moment and not worry about the future…

'If you really don't like the suit, Jack,' she told him, 'then change back into your old clothes.'

His eyes widened as he stared at her uncertainly. 'But I came here in a ripped T-shirt and dirty jeans.'

'I know.' She smiled conspiratorially at him. 'But so what? These journalists and photographers see slick, sophisticated people all day, every day. They are all about the curated image, the so-called authentic self that is absolutely anything but. Maybe you need to give them the real deal—who you truly are, warts and all.'

'Thankfully, I don't have any warts, but I take your meaning,' Jack replied, and she laughed.

'Well, phew, I guess.'

'Albert told me you'd give me a whole new image,' he told her thoughtfully. 'And you did, but now you're saying to scrap it?'

'Essentially, yes. I'm not trying to talk myself out of a job, but what's the point of being fake?'

'Well, it's a form of self-protection, I suppose,' Jack replied seriously. 'If you're fake, you can't be truly rejected, because the real you is never seen.'

'Exactly,' Lana answered, heartened that he got it—and, amazingly, finally, so did she. 'And what's the point of that? If you can't be real, what are you?'

'You are not,' Jack told her, 'sounding like a PR person.'

'I know.' Lana couldn't keep from laughing again. 'Maybe I need a rebranding. "Authentic PR" or something.'

Jack nodded slowly. 'That's not a bad idea.' Already he was shimmying out of the tight-fitting blazer. 'Now let me get out of this straitjacket.'

Lana was still smiling as she took a cab home later that evening. Jack had changed back into his old clothes, and given a very candid, very geeky interview that had completely surprised and charmed the journalist. The photographer had taken ruefully ironic photos of Jack, not looking smart and sleek, a superstar in the making, but doing goofy things, balancing a pencil on his nose or playing trashcan basketball. It was different and whimsical, and Lana was pretty sure he was going to be a huge hit with the public…and it had nothing to do with her.

'Why are you smiling like the cat who has the cream?' Christos asked when she came home. They had an evening charity gala to attend, and, while Lana usually looked forward to such events, she realised tonight she'd rather curl up at home with Christos and Netflix.

'I did something different today,' she said, and

then told him all about Jack Philips. 'I'm afraid I may be talking myself out of a career.'

'Or into an even better one, at least for a little while,' Christos replied as he pressed a kiss to her bump. They'd had the twenty-week scan six weeks ago, and the baby was healthy and growing; they'd decided not to find out whether it was a girl or boy.

'Some things,' Christos had said, 'are meant to be a surprise.'

'How's Junior today?' he asked as he straightened from greeting their baby to press a kiss on her lips.

'Fine. Making me a bit achy, so he or she must be growing.' She rubbed her bump ruefully; now that she wasn't working, she was conscious of the twinges in her back, along her belly. They'd been bothering her all day, but her OB had told her it was to be expected as the baby grew, and her muscles were forced to stretch.

Christos frowned in concern. 'We can skip tonight, if you'd rather.'

She would rather, but she knew it was an important event for him; he was about to close on a deal with a tech start-up he was interested in. 'No, let's go,' she told him. 'But maybe leave early.'

He caught her in his arms for another kiss and a devilish wag of his eyebrows. 'I'm always up for leaving early.'

Christos watched their limo pull to the kerb from the brownstone's balcony as he waited for Lana to emerge. He felt almost buoyant with happiness—as he had, amazingly, since that night when he'd confessed everything to her and she'd taken it in her stride, offered him acceptance and love in return.

Wait, *love*?

Christos let the knowledge spread inside him, as warm and golden as honey. Yes, *love*. In the end, it was just a word. He thought he'd probably loved Lana for a while—maybe even since she'd first slid onto the stool next to him and ordered a Snake Bite, and he'd been so impressed with her attitude, grit, and determination. That initial feeling had only grown in strength and certainty since then.

That first feeling was, perhaps, why he had been willing to agree to the paper marriage at the start, and then the pregnancy clause made three years later. It was why he hadn't been willing to embark on affairs, and why he wanted nothing more now than her in his arms, by his side, for ever.

The knowledge, surprisingly, didn't scare him. Was that what love did to you? Changed you? Made you into a better, stronger version of yourself?

But what if you let her down?

Admittedly, in the last three months, since that heartbroken confession, they hadn't engaged in that much emotional heavy lifting. Lana had told him a little bit about her childhood, the mother who had always been angry and distant, but she'd also said she'd made peace with it and forgiven her mother before she'd died. Telling him hadn't been so much about showing vulnerability as demonstrating how it was possible to move on from hard and painful things, and yet the fact that she had showed such vulnerability had made him love her *more*, not less.

But what about when the rubber hit the road? When life got hard, when things became uncertain or risky or dangerous? Would he be strong enough to love her then, the way he knew he wanted to?

Because he didn't have a great track record.

'I'm ready.'

Lana's voice floated from the living room and Christos turned, catching his breath at the sight of her. She looked glorious, in a floaty gown of emerald-green satin that draped over her bump and swirled about her calves and ankles. Her hair was drawn up in a loose bun, with tendrils curling about her face.

'I don't look like a tank in this, do I?' she asked with an uncertain laugh, and he strode forward to take her in his arms.

'You look like a goddess. Athena, as I once thought.'

She gave a little laugh back before he kissed her. 'Athena and not bodacious Venus?'

'Athena, goddess of wisdom. Smart and strong and a little bit intimidating but also incredibly lovely.' He kissed her again and for a second she rested in his arms, her head tucked beneath his chin.

'I'm so happy,' she said quietly, almost as if she was afraid of his response, or at least cautious of it. They'd skated on the surface these last few months, enjoying everything in a way that had felt easy, but after his confession on the balcony they hadn't gone any deeper. Was it because they hadn't needed to, or because they hadn't dared?

'I'm happy, too,' Christos replied in the same quiet tone.

Lana eased back to gaze up at him, her eyes wide and clear. 'I'm glad.'

It felt as if they were saying so much more than they actually were, and the import of the moment wasn't lost on him.

I can't disappoint her, he thought with a frisson of panic. *I can't let this lovely woman down, the way I did my own mother and sister. I have to be strong enough this time.*

Was it enough to want that, he wondered, even if he still wasn't sure he could?

An hour later they were circulating through the ballroom of one of the city's finest hotels, in fact the same hotel where Lana had first suggested the pregnancy clause to their marriage. Christos smiled to think of her then, so nervous and determined, and with that outrageous suggestion of IVF! He could laugh about it, now that he was gazing at her across the ballroom, laughing and chatting to someone, ripe with his child. Pride and, yes, *love* swelled within him. He loved her. He loved her. And he needed to tell her so.

'Hello, Christos.'

Christos turned at the sound of the quiet voice, his mouth dropping open when he saw who was standing in front of him, smiling sadly. His sister Sophia.

'Sophia…what are you doing here?'

'I came with a date. I don't often go to these big events, but occasionally I do.'

'I've never seen you…'

'No, but then you weren't looking.' She spoke pragmatically but Christos felt shame pierce him all the same. Sophia had lived just outside the city for years and he'd never made the effort, because it had always been easier not to. Not to face the memories, feel the guilt.

'I'm sorry,' he said, and she raised her eyebrows, her smile turning wry.

'What for?'

A gusty breath escaped him. 'For everything, I suppose. Not being there back…then, and not really since, either.' He shook his head. 'It was just always easier. For me, but also, I convinced myself, for you.' He paused, realising he'd never spoken so honestly to his sister before. 'But maybe it wasn't.'

She nodded slowly. 'We always wanted you there, Christos.'

'I know.' He realised as he said the words that he *did* know. It was all part of the guilt he'd felt, all the while trying not to feel it. Doing his best to believe that it was better for his family for him not to be around, when all the time it had been better for him. Although no, not better, just easier.

Except there had been nothing easy about it.

'I just couldn't bear to see your disappointment,' he confessed to Sophia in a low voice. 'And Dad… I know he still can't look me in the eye.'

Surprise flashed across his sister's face. 'Christos, it's you who can't look him in the eye. Dad doesn't blame you for anything.'

Christos shook his head, the movement visceral and instinctive. 'No, he does. Of course he does. I didn't—I didn't say goodbye to Mom. And I didn't look after all of you.'

'You were sixteen. He never should have asked you that, and he knows it, trust me.' She laid a hand on his arm. 'Talk to him, Christos. Talk to all of us.'

'Thalia…' Her name came thickly from his throat, tears stinging his eyes. He'd let down Thalia worst of all.

'Thalia has always had her issues,' Sophia told him. 'I know you've torn yourself into shreds over not coming when she asked you to, but, Christos, there was always going to be something with Thalia. That's how she's wired.'

'But if I had come when she—'

'You can't be sure of that,' Sophia cut across him. 'And in any case, you need to let it go. Think of the future, not the past.'

Christos smiled faintly. 'That's more or less what Lana told me.'

'I like her,' Sophie replied frankly. 'I think she has the strength of spirit to take you on.'

He laughed then, with genuine humour. 'Touché.'

Sophia smiled. 'I mean it.'

'I know you do.' He smiled back, and for a moment, things between them felt normal, warm. This, Christos realised, was easy. It was the easiest of all, and it gave him a glimpse of what the past could have been, but, more importantly, *far* more importantly, what the future could be.

A ripple of alarm travelled over the crowd, intermingled with gasps. Christos turned to look, as did Sophia, both of them frowning in consternation.

'Is there a doctor here?' someone cried out, and someone else asked for somebody to call 911.

'What's going on?' Sophia exclaimed, but suddenly, instinctively, Christos knew. He pushed his way through the crowd, his heart starting to thud, until he caught sight of her, and froze, transfixed by the terrible sight, a thousand terrible memories tumbling through his mind.

Lana was crumpled on the ground, her beautiful gown stained with blood.

CHAPTER FIFTEEN

EVERYTHING WAS A BLUR—the lights, the people, the sounds of concern and alarm. All Lana could feel was the intense, excruciating pain, banding her stomach, screaming in her back, obliterating all rational thought.

She'd been feeling twinges on and off all evening and had been determined to ignore them. Stretching pains, she'd told herself. They were natural, her OB had said. She'd had a check-up just three weeks ago and everything had been absolutely fine. Everything *would* be absolutely fine, she insisted to herself, because nothing could go wrong now that she was so happy—and so was Christos. He'd told her so, and it had been the next best thing to the words she was trying not to be too eager to hear. *I love you.* They'd been singing out of her heart every day, but they'd never passed her lips, nor Christos's. But it didn't matter, Lana had told herself, because she *knew* Christos loved her, even if he couldn't articulate it.

In any case, the pain had grown worse, harder to ignore, and then, in the middle of a conversation, she'd felt a sudden gush of liquid and she'd doubled over, gasping with the pain that had banded her middle, more intense than ever before.

She'd heard gasps and cries from the people around her before she'd crumpled to the floor. She'd felt liquid between her thighs, seeping into her dress, and when she'd put her hand to it, her palm had come away smeared with bright red blood.

She'd let out a cry, and then a doctor was there, and they were loading her onto a stretcher, and there were the blurred faces of so many people surrounding her, looking scared and concerned, but no one looked familiar.

No one was Christos.

He would hate this, she realised as they carried her to the ambulance. This was his worst nightmare come to life—having to be fully present and available emotionally in a situation as painful and dangerous as this. Facing his deepest fear again, with higher stakes than ever before. This was when love was tested, refined by fire, and what Christos had always been afraid of. Why he'd avoided it…until now.

Why he wasn't here, by her side, caring for her and their baby?

Because Lana didn't see him among the faces in the crowd, and she rode in the ambulance alone, passing out halfway through the journey, coming to in an operating theatre, a surgeon peering at her closely.

'Lana Smith?'

'Yes…'

'Your baby is in distress, due to a placental abruption. We need to perform an emergency Caesarean section. Do you give your consent?'

She'd blinked up at him, too woozy to fully understand what he was saying. 'But…but I'm only twenty-six weeks along…'

'This is the only way to save your baby.' The doctor sounded grimly certain, and Lana tried to grab his hand, but found she was too weak.

'Where's my husband?' she asked, her voice a desperate, plaintive thread of sound. 'Where is Christos Diakos?'

The doctor shook his head. 'I'm sorry, I don't know where your husband is.' She let out a choked cry and he continued, 'Do you give your consent?'

'Yes…*yes*.'

That was the last thing she remembered.

Lana didn't know how much time had passed when she woke next, to a hazy blur of light and sound. She tried to blink the world into focus and found she couldn't. She tried to reach down to feel the reassuring bump of her baby, but she wasn't strong enough to move her hand. Terror gripped her hard, but then she fell back into unconsciousness, grateful to let the world slide away again.

When she woke again, the world was a little clearer—she saw she was in a hospital room, everything white and sterile, and she was completely alone. An array of monitors and machines were positioned next to her, a steady beeping from one of them the only sound in the room. Tears gathered in her eyes as she looked around for Christos, but she couldn't see him anywhere.

She opened her mouth to call for him, but her lips were cracked and dry and no sound came out. And what about her baby? With what felt like superhuman effort, Lana reached down to touch her bump—and found, to her shocked horror, that it wasn't there. She felt nothing but sagging, empty flesh, and she let out a moan, a sound of raw grief, utter terror. Where was her baby?

Where was Christos?

Lying there, in that bright, sterile room, with no baby or husband, she didn't think she'd ever felt more alone.

This is why you don't let yourself love people, she thought, closing her eyes against the room, the world. *Because it hurts so much when they let you down. They walk away.*

Just as Christos had been afraid he would.

The next time Lana awoke, a nurse was in the room, bustling about by her bed. She must have made some sound, for the woman turned to glance at her, smiling when she saw her eyes were open.

'You're awake! Well, isn't that good news?'

'What…?' Lana's voice was paper-thin, and she had to lick her lips to moisten them, except her mouth was so dry she couldn't.

'Here, honey,' the woman said kindly. 'Let me give you a sip of water.'

She helped Lana lift her head to sip from a straw, the cool liquid wetting her lips and sliding down her throat, providing immediate relief.

Lana sagged against the pillows with a groan. 'Where…where is my baby?' she asked in a croak.

'Your baby is fine,' the nurse assured her. 'She's in the neonatal unit, since she was born so early. She's tiny, just two pounds seven ounces, but she's a fighter. The doctors feel she's got a very good chance indeed.'

Lana closed her eyes in both relief and sorrow. *Two pounds...!* The tiniest scrap of humanity, and yet so very precious. A little girl. A tiny, tiny, precious girl.

'When you're a little stronger, someone can take you to see her,' the woman promised. 'But you've been in a bad way, I'm afraid, for over a week. You lost a lot of blood, and for a while…' She shook her head and Lana felt fear clutch at her.

Had she been that close to death? Christos would have been out of his mind with worry and fear…

Or maybe he hadn't been. Maybe he'd just walked away.

She didn't want to believe it, she couldn't, and yet the reality was stark, staring at her straight in her face. He wasn't here.

'Have you…?' Her voice rasped painfully in her throat, and she swallowed, determined to get the words out. 'Have you seen my husband?'

The nurse gave her a confused look, her forehead furrowed. 'Your husband? What does he look like?'

'Tall…dark hair…hazel eyes…'

The most handsome man in the world.

The nurse shook her head, sympathy now softening her features. 'I'm sorry, I don't think I've seen him. That doesn't mean he hasn't been here, though. I'm only on shift a couple of times a week…'

And she hadn't seen him about at all? No dutiful husband sitting by the bedside, then. Tears silently slipped down Lana's cheeks as she realised Christos must not have been there at all. Had he left her, left their daughter, just as he had his own family? And what did that say about *her*? Her father had left her when she'd been only a baby, her mother had resented her for her whole life, the one man she'd convinced herself she'd loved before had walked away without a single care.

Why should Christos be any different? Why should she? They'd both just been conforming to their true selves. Lana would always be left…and Christos would always do the leaving.

'I'm sure he's here somewhere,' the nurse told her, patting her hand. 'It's a busy hospital…maybe he's with your daughter…' She trailed off, rather feebly, Lana thought, because if she'd been so ill for so long, surely Christos would have been there at some point. The nurse would have recognised the description, at least. 'I'll ask around,' the nurse said, and Lana let out a choked sound, something between a laugh and a sob.

'Don't bother,' she said. 'I don't want to see him.' And then she closed her eyes, trying to shut out the grim truth that she couldn't avoid; it screamed in her ears, seeped into every pore. Christos had left her.

'She doesn't want to see you.'

The nurse's expression was implacable as Christos stared at her in incredulity that quickly morphed into fury—and fear.

'What? What on earth do you mean?'

'I'm sorry, sir. Your wife made it very clear she didn't want to see you.'

Frustration burned in his chest, along with a far deeper hurt. Lana didn't want to see him?

Yet was he even that surprised?

He'd failed her, back at the ballroom. He'd failed her so badly. When he'd seen her lying there, crumpled on the ground, everything in him had shut down. He'd been incapable of thought, of movement, frozen in place by the memories that had tormented him for so many years—his mother in her bed, calling out to him. Thalia's broken voice on the phone. The way he'd failed before, and the utter terror that it was happening again.

He would let Lana down.

He already had. And yet he still couldn't make himself move.

He'd stood there, completely frozen with terror, with memory, while she'd been bundled onto a stretcher, taken away. Then Sophia had touched his shoulder, squeezed.

'Christos, it's going to be okay. We'll go to the hospital.'

He'd stared at his sister blankly, and then it was

as if he'd had an injection of adrenaline, of realisation. He had to get to Lana. He wouldn't fail her any more than he already had. By the time he'd made it outside of the hotel, she'd already been on the way to the hospital.

What must she have thought, when she'd looked around in those frightening moments, and hadn't seen him?

He'd known he would hate the fact that he'd disappointed her in those crucial moments, but he'd also known he had to look forward…for the sake of their marriage, their child. By the time he had arrived at the hospital with Sophia, having been told Lana was taken to a different one, she was already in the operating theatre, having an emergency C-section. Christos had been powerless to do anything but wait.

And then he'd received the news that Lana had had a little girl, a tiny baby girl who had been fighting for her life…as Lana had been fighting for her own. He'd stared at the surgeon in blank shock as he'd removed his surgical mask, looking weary and almost as hopeless as Christos had felt.

'It was a placental abruption. These are very rare, happening in less than one per cent of all pregnancies, but when they do happen, they're sudden and very dangerous.'

Christos had felt his stomach hollowing out while Sophia had stood next to him, a steadying presence. 'What…?' He'd had to make himself start again. 'What are you saying?'

'Your wife lost a lot of blood, Mr Diakos. A *lot* of blood. She's being given a transfusion, but when a patient has lost as much blood as she has, it's always a cause for concern. A grave cause for concern.'

'Are you saying her life is in danger?' Christos had demanded hoarsely.

The surgeon had nodded grimly. 'That's exactly what I'm saying.'

Christos's reaction had been visceral and immediate. 'Let me see her. I have to see her.'

'I'm sorry, but that won't be possible just now. When she's more stable, yes. But until then…'

'I have to see her,' Christos had insisted, his voice rising, his fists clenching. 'You don't understand—'

'Mr Diakos, I understand completely,' the surgeon had replied wearily. 'But until the transfusion is complete and we can be sure that her body has accepted the new blood, seeing her could put her in danger. I promise you, as soon as it is safe, you will see her.'

Safe had been an endless eighteen hours. He'd insisted Sophia go home; she'd promised to return in the morning. She'd been there for him in a way he hadn't been for her, in the past, and he'd been painfully grateful for it. Meanwhile, Christos hadn't slept, hadn't eaten, hadn't done anything but panic and pray. He'd also seen their daughter, their tiny baby girl, so perfect and pink and small, the most beautiful baby that had ever lived. If he'd been allowed, he could have held her in the palm of one hand. As it was, he'd had to make do with peering at her through the glass, his heart aching and aching. He could lose the two people he loved most in the world…and what he knew most of all was he was going to be there for them. This time, he was going to be there for both of them.

When they'd finally let him see Lana, she'd been unconscious, her beautiful face so very pale, her body so terribly still. He'd held her hand and talked to her, tried to make her laugh even though he'd known she couldn't hear him.

'That first time you sat next to me in that bar, Lana? I fell for you then.' He'd almost been able to hear her scoff, and he'd continued as if they were actually having a conversation. 'I'm serious. I didn't realise it, of course. I'm not that sentimental. But I fell for you—for your strength and your spirit, but also because of the vulnerability I glimpsed underneath, although if someone had told me as much, I would have run a mile. You know I would have, don't you? You always sensed that about me, even before I told you as much. But not now, Lana.' His voice had choked, and he'd stroked her hand, trying to keep the tears at bay. 'I'm not running now. I never will again.'

At other times, he'd spoken to her of their daughter. 'She's the most beautiful thing you've ever seen. Tiny but fierce. She certainly has your spirit, thank goodness. All the doctors and nurses say she's a fighter. She's going to fight for her life, Lana, and so are you.' Again, his voice had broken and this time he'd had to pass a hand over his face, exhausted, overwhelmed, *emotional*. 'You are,' he'd insisted. 'I know you are. You have to, Lana, for our baby girl, and—and for me. Because I love you. I should have said those words before, because heaven knows I've felt them for so long. But I love you. *I love you.*'

With every fibre of his being, he'd willed her to open her eyes, to hear him, but she'd slept on, as beautiful as an angel, as still as a statue. Then their baby girl had developed a fever, and for two days he'd gone between their bedsides, afraid for both of their lives, while Sophia had supplied him with takeaway meals and decent cups of coffee from a nearby café.

When their daughter was finally out of the danger zone—for now—he'd gone back to Lana, only to be told by this stony-faced nurse that his wife didn't want to see him.

For a second, Christos hadn't been able to process it, because he'd just been so glad that Lana was finally awake and able to speak. But what the hell did she mean, she didn't want to see him?

And yet was he even surprised?

'There must be a mistake,' he insisted, trying his best to keep his voice level when in truth he felt like shouting, swearing, storming into Lana's room, and yet at the same time weeping from his own guilt and grief. 'My wife will want to see me,' he said, wanting to believe it. 'I know she will.'

'She said she didn't.'

'Look,' Christos said, and now his voice was wavering, trembling. 'It's been an incredibly intense week. Lana—my wife—was in danger of losing her life, and our baby girl was, as well. Whatever she's saying…it might be she doesn't realise what's going on. What's happened. I need to see her.'

The nurse's expression softened briefly. 'She did ask for you,' she admitted. 'And seemed disappointed when you weren't there.'

Which was a knife to the heart if anything was. Christos practically staggered. So Lana knew he'd let her down. How could he possibly make it up to her? 'Please let me see her,' he said quietly, a plea, and thankfully, *thankfully*, the nurse finally nodded.

Seconds later he was opening the door to Lana's room, holding his breath as he saw his wife half sitting up in bed, still looking so pale, her eyes closed. They opened when he closed the door, awareness flaring in their crystalline depths, and then, to his surprise, to his sorrow, Lana began to cry.

He'd never seen her cry before, not like this. Her expression seemed to collapse in on itself and her shoulders shook as she held her hands up to her face, as if to hide her tears, her pain.

'Lana. Lana. My darling Lana.'

He went to the bed and took her gently in his arms, kissing her hair, her hands, and then her damp cheeks when she let him. He didn't even hear what he was saying, over and over again, until Lana, through her tears, asked, 'Do you really mean that?'

Then he realised he'd been saying, over and over, *I love you.*

'Yes,' he told her. 'I love you. I love you. You've given me the biggest scare of my life this last week, but I love you so much. So, so much. More than anything, except perhaps our baby daughter, who is the most gorgeous thing in the world, save you.' He kissed her again as she laughed brokenly, through her tears.

'Is she all right?'

'She's going to be all right,' he stated firmly. 'And I'll take you to see her as soon as they let me. She has your spirit, Lana, and your blue eyes.'

She laughed again, a hiccup of sound. 'Christos, every baby has blue eyes.'

'Not as blue as yours,' he returned, and she smiled, although she still looked tearful, and that made him ache, because he knew it was his doing, and he'd never wanted to be the one to hurt her.

'I thought you'd gone,' she said quietly, a confession. 'I thought… I thought you'd left me. For good.'

'Never.' He held her face in his hands as he gazed into her eyes, wanting to imbue her with his certainty, his strength of feeling. 'Never, Lana. When you first…collapsed, back at the hotel, I wasn't able to get to you in time. I'm so, so sorry. You were in the ambulance, being whisked away, before I could.' He paused, knowing he needed to be completely honest. 'I froze,' he said in a low voice. 'For just a few seconds. It all came rushing back—with my mother, with Thalia, my *fear*, and I couldn't move. I couldn't do anything. But only for a moment, Lana, I swear.' But a terrible moment too long. He knew that. 'I'm sorry,' he whispered. 'So sorry.'

'Oh, Christos—'

'By the time I ran towards you, you were in the ambulance. And then they told me the wrong hospital, and by the time I got to you, you were in Theatre. But as soon as I could see you, sit with you, I did. I was. I swear, Lana.' He squeezed her hands, desperate for her to believe him, for her sake as well as his own. 'I let you down. I know I did, and I'm sorry. But I swear I never will again.'

'A nurse told me she hadn't seen you,' Lana whispered. 'And when I woke up, you weren't there.'

'I'm so sorry—'

'It's not your fault.' She shook her head, squeezing his hands back. 'It was just…for a moment, it felt like all my old fears came to the fore. All the insecurities I never let myself think about, never mind admit to anyone else. I thought about my mother, my father, the man I…' She gulped. 'And I wondered why I was even surprised that you would leave me, when everyone I'd cared about had left me before—'

He couldn't bear to hear her say such things, and yet he knew she'd needed to say them. 'Oh, Lana.'

'I should have been more honest before, about how…vulnerable I felt, I suppose. I didn't even realise quite how much until you were gone. But even so, I should have trusted you, Christos.' Her eyes were wide, filled with both pain and regret. 'I should have believed you would be there, if you could. It was just for a little while it felt as if I couldn't even think—'

'I understand,' he whispered, because of course he did. 'And I'm so sorry.'

'It doesn't matter.' She smiled, although her eyes still held the pearly sheen of tears. 'You're here now. I'm so sorry I doubted you, even for a moment.'

He shook his head, his throat thick with emotion. 'And I'm so sorry I gave you reason to doubt.'

'You didn't, Christos. It was me…my fear and insecurity.'

'Still.'

'No more looking back at the past,' she reminded him. 'Only to the future…a future where we're together.'

He nodded almost fiercely. 'Always.'

Her expression became serious as she continued, 'I should have said those words earlier too, Christos, because I love you. I love you so much. I didn't want to, I fought against it, but it happened anyway.' She laughed, wiping the last of her tears, as he took her in his arms again.

'I'm glad,' he told her. 'I am very, very glad.'

With a small, impish smile curving her lips, Lana leaned back to look up at him. 'Three points regarding our marriage,' she stated, eyebrows lifted in query.

Christos grinned, before making a show of frowning in thought. 'Let's see…first point, I love you.'

'Second point, I love you,' she fired back.

'And third point, we love our daughter.'

Her smile turned satisfied as she nodded slowly. 'I

like the sound of those points,' she said, and Christos kissed her again.

'Me too,' he replied as he took her in his arms, and she nestled against him. 'Me too.'

EPILOGUE

Three years later

'LOOK AT ME, Mama, look at me!'

'I'm looking, darling, I'm looking,' Lana replied with a laugh as her daughter, Charis Marina, ran down the hill, blonde curls flying. They had named her Charis, the Greek word for grace, because it had felt fitting. So much grace had been shown, in the midst of all the heartache and healing. And Marina, for Christos's mother, so she would always be remembered.

Those first few months after Charis's birth had been challenging, to say the least. She'd stayed in the hospital for four months, and Lana had gone there every day to hold her daughter, to drip-feed her from an eye dropper, to make sure her daughter, tiny as she was, knew she was loved. Christos had come in the evenings, and sometimes during his lunch hour, and somehow, they'd survived—two fevers, a bout of pneumonia, and some serious jaundice, but Charis had come home when she was four and a half months old, weighing just over four pounds.

Since then, she'd continued to grow and strengthen, a little behind her peers in terms of physical development, and definitely on the petite side, but the paediatrician had said that was normal. She was their little sprite, with her blue eyes—the same colour as Lana's, just as Christos had predicted—and her wild blonde locks.

She'd brought Christos's family together in a way they never had been before; this new life had created a new life for the family—one of forgiveness and acceptance. Now she and Christos regularly made the trip out to Brookhaven to see his father and sisters; Thalia, although still fragile, adored her little niece, and Kristina delighted in being an auntie, sneaking Charis treats from her bakery whenever she could. Sophia, living so close to the city, had become a regular visitor to their home there, as well as here, the sprawling, relaxed house they'd bought out in the Hamptons, for weekends and summers. Lana loved nothing more than running through the long grass with her daughter, or looking for shells on the beach, or baking—something she'd never done before—with Charis dipping her finger into whatever she was mixing, no matter Lana's gentle reprimands.

'But it's so good, Mama,' she'd protest, making Lana smile.

She'd taken to motherhood in a way she'd never

thought possible, in part because the nature of Charis's birth had made her daughter all the more precious. Her condition meant she wouldn't have any more children, although she and Christos had spoken about adoption, and they'd had their first meeting with a caseworker just last week. It felt as if all things were possible, because they'd already seen and survived so much.

They were here, after all.

'Careful, sprite!' In one easy armful, Christos scooped up a squealing Charis and tossed her over his shoulder as he strolled towards Lana, lying on a picnic blanket on the grass. It was a beautiful summer's day, the sky the colour of a robin's egg, the sunshine lemony and warm. A day that felt like a blessing, like so much in their lives.

'There you go.' He deposited Charis onto the blanket, and their daughter scrambled up and threw herself into Lana's arms, who accepted her with a startled *oof* before drawing her into a hug.

'Hello, pumpkin,' she murmured against her hair. Her gaze met Christos's over their daughter's head and they shared a loving, tender smile. Lana knew what he was thinking without him having to say it, because she was thinking it, too.

Are you as happy as I am? As thankful? As blessed?

The three points regarding their family.

With a smile, Lana settled their daughter between them and leaned over to kiss her husband. Yes, the three points of their family, and the only ones she needed to remember. As she met Christos's smiling gaze once more, she knew he was thinking it, too.

*****

Did the chemistry in
Pregnancy Clause in Their Paper Marriage
knock you off your feet?
If so, you'll love these other
Kate Hewitt stories!

The Italian's Unexpected Baby
Vows to Save His Crown
Pride and the Italian's Proposal
A Scandal Made at Midnight
Back to Claim His Italian Heir

Available now!

COMING NEXT MONTH FROM

HARLEQUIN
PRESENTS

#4185 THE SECRET OF THEIR BILLION-DOLLAR BABY

Bound by a Surrogate Baby

by Dani Collins

Sasha married billionaire Rafael Zamos to escape her stepfather's control. But is the gilded cage of her convenient union any better? Lost within their marital facade, Sasha fiercely protects her heart while surrendering to her husband's intoxicating touch… Might a child bring them closer?

#4186 THE KING'S HIDDEN HEIR

by Sharon Kendrick

Emerald Baker was a cloakroom attendant when she spent one mind-blowing night with a prince. Now Konstandin is a king—and he insists that Emmy marry him when she tells him he is a father! For the sake of her son, she'll consider his ruthlessly convenient proposal…

#4187 A TYCOON TOO WILD TO WED

The Teras Wedding Challenge

by Caitlin Crews

All innocent Brita Martis craves is freedom from her grasping family, and marrying powerful Asterion Teras may be her best chance of escape. The chemistry that burns between them at first sight thrills her, but when their passion explodes, she is lost! Unless she can tame the wildest tycoon of all…

#4188 TWIN CONSEQUENCES OF THAT NIGHT

by Pippa Roscoe

When billionaire Nate Harcourt jets to Spain on business, he runs straight into his electrifying one-night stand from two years ago. Except Gabi Casas now has twins—his heirs! His childhood as an orphan taught Nate to trust nobody, but he wants better for his sons… so he drops to one knee!

HPCNMRA0224

#4189 CONTRACTED AND CLAIMED BY THE BOSS

Brooding Billionaire Brothers

by Clare Connelly

Former child star Paige Cooper now shuns fame and works as a nanny. When Australian pearl magnate and single father Max Stone hires her to help his daughter, she's shocked by her red-hot response to him. And as the days count down on Paige's contract, resistance is futile...

#4190 SAYING "I DO" TO THE WRONG GREEK

The Powerful Skalas Twins

by Tara Pammi

Ani's wedding will unlock her trust fund and grant her freedom—she just doesn't expect infuriatingly attractive Xander at the altar! Penniless, Ani can't afford to walk away. Their craving for each other might be as hot as her temper, but can she risk falling for a man who scorns love?

#4191 A DIAMOND FOR HIS DEFIANT CINDERELLA

by Lorraine Hall

Matilda Willoughby's guardian, ultra-rich Javier Alatorre, is determined to marry her off before her twenty-fifth birthday. Otherwise he must marry her himself! As she clashes with him at every turn, her burning hatred soon becomes scorching need. And Matilda is unprepared for how thin the line between love and hate really is!

#4192 UNDONE IN THE BILLIONAIRE'S CASTLE

Behind the Billionaire's Doors...

by Louise Fuller

Ivo Faulkner has a business deal to close. Except after his explosive night with Joan Santos, his infamous laser focus is nowhere to be found! He invites her to his opulent castle to exorcise their attraction, but by indulging their temptation, Ivo risks being unable to ever let his oh-so-tempting Cinderella go...